CHRISTIE RIDGWAY

Native Californian Christie Ridgway started reading and writing romances in middle school. It wasn't until she was the wife of her college sweetheart and the mother of two small sons that she submitted her work for publication. Many contemporary romances later, she is happiest when telling her stories despite the splash of kids in the pool, the mass of cups and plates in the kitchen and the many commitments she makes in the world beyond her desk.

Besides loving the men in her life and her dream-come-true job, she continues her long-time love affair with reading and is never without a stack of books. You can find out more about Christie or contact her at her website, www.christieridgway.com

To firefighters
and all first responders who dedicate
their lives to saving ours.

Runaway Bride Returns!

CHRISTIE RIDGWAY

First published in Great Britain 2009
Large Print edition 2010
Harlequin Mills & Boon Limited,
Eton House, 18-24 Paradise Road,
Richmond, Surrey TW9 1SR

© Christie Ridgway 2009

ISBN: 978 0 263 21614 1

Harlequin Mills & Boon policy is to use papers that
are natural, renewable and recyclable products and
made from wood grown in sustainable forests. The
logging and manufacturing process conform to the legal
environmental regulations of the country of origin.

Printed and bound in Great Britain
by CPI Antony Rowe, Chippenham, Wiltshire

Chapter One

If Owen Marston hadn't already been flat on his back in a hospital bed, he might have been tempted to knock himself out so he didn't have to deal with the family members gathered around him. Less than twenty-four hours had passed since he'd been admitted, and already he couldn't wait to get out of this place with its pink plastic pitchers and beeping machinery. He craved time alone, but he was managing to keep it together okay, mostly by pretending he wasn't here and by pretending that what actually had happened had not.

To that end, he tuned out his mother's conversation and thought of his spacious condo, his big bed, his large-screen TV. Solitude. God, he needed it.

"And your hair still smells like smoke," his mother said, the anxious edge of her voice breaking into his reverie. Her fingers worried the pearls at her throat. "Caro, don't you think your brother's hair still smells like smoke?"

"Mom," Caro replied, her voice patient. "It doesn't matter that Owen's hair smells like smoke. It's no big deal that the thread count on the sheets isn't up to snuff, and that the pattern of the curtains is an offense to anyone with taste. This is a hospital, not a hotel, a resort or a spa. We're interested in Owen getting good health care, not concierge service."

Their mother ignored his sister's points to appeal to Owen's younger brother. "Bryce, don't you think your brother's hair smells like smoke?"

The woman was seriously losing it. Bryce didn't seem bothered by the fact, though. Sprawled in a nearby chair, he kept his attention focused on his iPhone. Maybe he was checking the latest sports scores, though more likely he was poring over some financials e-mailed to him by his assistant.

Their mother huffed out a sigh. "Bryce, are you listening—"

"Call for you, Owen," his brother said. "Granddad on speaker phone." He slid the device onto the fake woodgrain surface of the plastic table pulled up to Owen's bed.

Owen glared at Bryce, who just shrugged as their grandfather's used-to-smoke-a-pack-a-day voice carried into the room. "Boy, I just heard you're in the hospital. How come nobody told me this yesterday?"

Owen looked around. His father, who had a minute ago been standing at the foot of his bed, was now gone, just another in his long string of well-practiced disappearing acts that he managed to make each time the elder Marston started in with his demands. His mother had her back turned now and was murmuring with Caro. In a convenient blink of an eye, Bryce was immersed in some paperwork he'd pulled from his briefcase.

Owen glanced toward the doorway again. A slim, feminine figure flitted past. His body jerked, his attention lasering on the fluttering ends of dark hair and the receding echo of stiletto heels.

Wait! Was that…? Could it be…?

His heart pounded and he shifted, struggling to lift up, but his ankle, his arm, his head and every muscle he had protested. Collapsing back to the pillow, he tried telling himself to take it easy. It couldn't have been her. Why would she show up now? And he wouldn't want her to, that was for damn sure, not when he felt as if he'd been rolled downhill in a barrelful of rocks.

His grandfather's voice sounded louder

through the phone's speaker. "Why didn't anyone tell me yesterday?" Philip Marston demanded again.

Owen's gaze stayed focused on the empty doorway, and though tension still grabbed at his gut, he managed to keep his words even and calm. "Nobody told you yesterday, Granddad, because there was nothing definitive to tell until today. And today we knew you were locked in meetings with the governor all morning and afternoon."

"Well, I want a full report right now, young man. What the hell happened?"

"A little bump on the head, a little smoke inhalation and I broke my ulna." His sister had convinced him to go with royal blue for the cast that ran from hand to elbow, and it looked stupid to Owen now, but he felt even stupider for the way his heart had sped up when he imagined that feminine figure in the doorway. Especially since what he'd once thought he'd felt for that woman had been a figment of his imagination, too.

"And then I sprained my right ankle and broke my left foot." Thank God no cast on that one, just one of those big ugly boots.

"I warned you," Philip Marston said, his tone disapproving. "I warned you that this so-called career you've chosen was no good."

Owen's tension tightened, clamping on his lungs like a vise, but he didn't surrender a groan, much less a sigh. "Yes, Granddad, so you did."

"I'm glad you concede that," the old man grumbled.

Owen's chest squeezed tighter and acid burned in his belly.

"And I predicted—"

"You never once predicted this, damn it," Owen heard himself snap. Chest still painfully tight, he spoke right over his grandfather's raspy voice as a tirade he hadn't known was in him broke free. "You never predicted I'd fall through the roof of a two-story house."

"Owen—"

"You said I'd get bored, you said I was wasting my college education, you said I was turning my back on the family business. But admit you never once forecasted this, Granddad. You never once declared I'd find myself in a hospital bed, my body busted all to pieces, and—"

"Owen—"

"—and one of my best buddies dead."

On that last word—*dead*—Owen's outburst came to an abrupt halt. *Dead.*

Unable to draw a full breath, he ignored the sputter coming through the phone's speaker and thumbed off the gadget before tossing it to his brother, who was staring at him.

His mother was staring, too. His sister. His father had ventured into the room again and was looking at Owen with alarm, as well.

Of course they all looked alarmed. He knew why. It was because he was usually laid-back. Calm in a crisis. Impervious to pressure, and he'd withstood a hell of a lot of it to go his own way and become a firefighter instead of some dull suit in the

Marston business empire. But crap, last night had been a disaster, and not only had his body betrayed him by breaking up in his fall, but now his imagination was playing tricks on him, too.

She was nowhere nearby.

"Ross," his mother said to his father. "Go out there and track down that doctor. It's time we get Owen released from this place. I think the atmosphere isn't doing him any good."

June Marston probably was certain it was the curtains that were making him surly, but what did he care? Getting out sounded terrific. His quiet, spacious condo sounded perfect.

"I want him home," his mother continued, "where I can keep an eye on him."

Now the alarmed one was Owen. His gaze

shot toward his mom. "Home? Home, as in *your* home? No thanks, Mom."

"Owen—"

"Dad." He pinned his father with his gaze, though the older man appeared about a "hocus-pocus" away from going invisible again. "Just get me back to my condo. That's all I want." That and to turn back the clock twenty-four hours. Or, hell, if he was making wishes, there was a whole other day he'd like to undo, as well, just over a month ago, in Las Vegas, when a certain woman had high-heeled into his life.

His father cleared his throat. "Your mother may be right, Owen. How are you going to get around, hobbled like you are? Your condo's three stories, with the bedroom a flight of steps from the kitchen."

It didn't matter. He'd be dead before he—

Oh, God. There was that word again. *Dead.* Last night the world had turned to fiery hell, and when the flames finally subsided, Jerry Palmer was dead.

Jerry Palmer was dead.

From a dark place deep inside him, something cold welled up to wash over Owen's body. His stomach pitched and a clammy sweat broke over his flesh as tension tightened again around his chest.

How had this happened? Why had he lived when Jerry was dead? He closed his eyes, trying to get away from the question. Trying to get away, period.

"Ross." His mother's voice was distant. "I really think you need to find the doctor. Or maybe we just require some sort of administrator type to get the paperwork going to get Owen home."

Home. Hell, that's where he was going, no matter what noises his mother made. His home, here in Paxton, where he could hole up and lick his wounds and lock the door against the world, including his well-meaning but never-understood-him-anyway relatives.

His eyes were still closed when he heard a change in the pitch of his mother's voice. "Oh, wonderful. Young lady, are you here about my son Owen? I certainly hope so, as we'd like to expedite getting him out of here."

"Yes, I am here about Owen," a voice replied.

A voice he knew. A voice he'd been dreaming of since that weekend in Las Vegas. *Her* voice. His heart started pounding again and he felt the bruises riddling his body begin to throb.

She *was* here. Now. Why?

Why now, when it was five weeks ago that she'd stomped off following their argument in Vegas? Why now, when she hadn't contacted him since? But wasn't it just like her confounding, inconvenient self to show up today, as he was lying in a hospital bed wearing a ridiculous blue cast and feeling like a 0.5 on a scale of 1 to 10?

And with hair that still smelled of smoke. He lifted his hand to his bristly cheek before he forced himself to lift his eyelids and take in the woman who had the gall to appear so damn beautiful from her place in the doorway.

She was small and sleek, her black hair a

shiny wing that curved to her throat. Her eyes were chocolate brown with lashes that were long and curled and that had brushed his throat when they danced—they'd been that close. Her skin was a flawless golden and her full lips the color of a plum. He'd kissed that mouth, nipped it, painted it with his tongue, lost himself in its sweet flavor.

He'd lost his head over those kisses. Over her.

"How are you, Izzy?" he asked, surprised to find that though his voice was roughened by the smoke inhalation, he wasn't growling like he wanted to.

"Better than you, I see," she said softly.

Her gaze trained on him, she took a step into the room and he crossed his arms over his chest, the stupid cast clunking against his breastbone. Izzy winced, her downturned mouth sympathetic. "Oh, Owen."

"'Oh, Owen,' what?" Damn, but he didn't want her feeling sorry for him. He wanted her…hell, he didn't want anything from her except one thing. And she was a flight risk, she'd proven that, so he knew what he had to do now that she'd ventured this close again.

Busted up or not, feeling about as weak as skim milk or not, he must do anything, say anything, agree to anything that would strong-arm her into sticking around long enough to solve the untenable situation they'd put themselves in five weeks before. He couldn't let her run away again.

It was Caro who reminded them both that there were other people in the room. She bounced up from her chair with a smile and held out her hand. "I'm Owen's sister, Caro."

Izzy returned a polite shake. "And I'm…" She glanced over at Owen, obviously asking for help.

He made a little gesture with his hand. "Caro, meet Isabella Cavaletti. Izzy, also meet my brother, Bryce, and my parents, June and Ross."

Handshakes were exchanged all around and then he gave his family one last piece of info to chew on. Might as well, since he now had this on his plate, too.

"Everybody," he said to the other Marstons in the room. "Meet my wife."

Izzy's plan hadn't been well formed. If forced to articulate it, she might have mumbled something about wanting a quick peek to reassure herself Owen was okay. As if a 3,000-mile flight for a single quick peek made any kind of sense.

And anyway, that quick peek had turned into a hover-in-the-doorway the instant she'd caught sight of the cast on his arm, the elastic bandages on his ankle, and the other foot in some sort of device that signaled an additional injury. She couldn't help but take in the dishevelment of his dark blond hair, the scrape high on his cheekbone, and the cut across the bridge of his nose. A man had never looked, she'd decided, so weary and so gorgeous at the same time.

His battered appearance had frozen her in place and then she'd been spotted by a tall, beautiful older woman wearing patrician pearls and a worried expression. Owen's mother, June Marston.

She'd looked much happier when she thought Izzy was a hospital employee rather than her son's wife. That apparently put a sour taste in her mouth, because now she was staring at Izzy, her lips pursed and her eyes wide in surprise. "Wife?" she echoed.

Owen seemed unwilling to offer more, so Izzy sucked in a breath and gathered together her charm. By now, it came naturally to her, being friendly with strangers, getting them to like her and feel comfortable with her right away. She'd developed the skill out of necessity as a child, and the practice now aided her in her career.

"I'm a library consultant," she told Owen's family. She tried out an engaging smile, one she hoped would distract them from noticing she wasn't answering the wife question, even as she stole another look at Owen, trying to better assess his condition. Her hands had gone cold and her stomach ached. Should it hurt so much that *he* was hurt?

"I travel around the country visiting public library systems," she continued, "to help them modernize their services and increase their ease of use and popularity."

Owen's brother had risen to his feet when they'd been introduced and his interest seemed to kindle at the words *modernize* and *increase*. A business type, she guessed, taking in his gray suit and starched white dress shirt. "What kind of suggestions do you generally make?"

"Often I propose redesigning to make the library feel and look more like a big-chain bookstore. Comfortable easy chairs, displays of the current bestsellers, coffee bars. That sort of thing."

"Coffee bars." Bryce appeared intrigued. "Really."

"Ask her about the Dewey decimal system," Owen put in.

Izzy sent him a surprised glance. Maybe he was better than he appeared. Even one hundred percent injury-free, she wouldn't have thought he'd remember that. They hadn't spent a lot of time together in Las Vegas, and little of it had been focused on their jobs. Instead, their hours had been dedicated to sweet and deep drugging kisses, to memorizing the lines of each other's bodies with sensuous touches that could turn urgent even when they were only swaying together on a dance floor.

"Okay, I'll bite," Bryce said, derailing the dangerous train of her thoughts. "What about the Dewey decimal system?"

She slid another look at Owen. "Well…"

"The day I met her, she was coming off a five-day librarians' convention wearing a round badge that read 'Dewey' with a red slash through it."

Bryce's face—less rugged than Owen's, but not less handsome—lit up with his boyish grin. "No Dewey decimal system?"

It was what labeled her a rebel in bibliophile circles. She was a heretic to some for her views on the archaic cataloging system. "I advocate shelving books in 'neighborhoods' based on subject matter. It makes more sense to patrons and is easier for them to use."

Bryce seemed to like the idea. "You must be a very persuasive and busy woman."

"Busy? Yeah," Owen confirmed, his voice dry. "So busy it's been impossible for her to call her—"

"Husband?" June Marston said, blinking as if coming out of a coma. "Wife? The two of you are really married?"

Owen grimaced, looking to Izzy as if he were regretting spilling the secret. His mother rushed toward his bed, apparently interpreting his expression differently. "Owen, what's wrong? Are you in more pain? What do you need?"

Owen flicked another glance at Izzy, then

directed his gaze back to his mother. "Look, Mom, I'll explain the married thing later. But right now what I really need is some peace and quiet." He shifted his shoulders on the pillow as if trying to get more comfortable. "Why don't you and everyone just go?"

That sounded perfect to Izzy. He could explain the married thing to his family at some later date and she'd come back when he was feeling better and they could be alone to discuss what she'd been avoiding the last five weeks. Maybe by then she'd have found some rational explanation for why she'd been AWOL all that time.

Ready to beat a hasty—if temporary—retreat, she went into an immediate back-pedal, deciding she'd locate a nearby hotel. From there, she could call her best friend,

Emily, the new librarian in this 'burg, and talk over the fastest way to fix this sticky predicament with the man she'd married on a whim in Las Vegas. Izzy's hip bumped into Owen's sister, Caro, who seemed to be guarding the door.

"'Everyone', Owen?" Caro asked.

"Everyone but—" he lifted his uninjured hand to point a forefinger at Izzy "—*you*."

The Marstons were a clan of tall people. Strong. Possibly domineering. Because one minute Izzy was near the door and the next she'd been herded by a slender blond Amazon—aka Caro—to Owen's bedside. There, he caught her fingers with those of his that stuck out of his bright blue cast. They were long, hard fingers, and as she stared down at the tangle they made with hers, she felt a jolt in her chest. A sting at the corners of her eyes.

Because…it must be because she didn't like to see him harmed in any way. Not because he was her husband, of course—that wasn't really real. She didn't like seeing him hurt because she was a woman and he was a man—no, because she was a *human being* and he was a human being, and that's the way that good human beings felt toward each other.

His fingers tightened on hers. "You shouldn't have run out on me," he murmured. "Why did you?"

Heat rushed up her neck. She *shouldn't* have run out on him. That's not the way good human beings treated each other, it was true. She'd known she couldn't ignore their marriage forever, she'd known she'd been wrong even as she'd used their brief but blistering argument as the impetus to leave him behind in Las Vegas, but could coming back here and doing this face-to-face make it right? "I heard you were calling my name in the ambulance," she heard herself whisper, avoiding another awkward question by posing one of her own. "Why did you?"

Before he could answer—would he answer?—Ross Marston stepped up beside her. "Son, before we go we have to get a few details ironed out."

Owen rubbed his free hand against his whiskered chin. "What details, Dad?"

"I can get your mother to leave quietly now if you'll agree to come to the penthouse in San Francisco to recover once the hospital releases you."

His fingers twitched, squeezing Izzy's and then easing up. "I can't—"

"You can't stay at home alone, either," his mother said, folding her arms over the silk jacket of her expensive-looking pantsuit. "Owen Marston, you've always been stubborn, but you're going to need family around you."

"Mom—"

"Owen. You can't take care of yourself, not while you have only one working limb." She turned to Izzy. "Surely as his…his… good friend, or whatever you are, you can help me convince him that he can't go home to his condo by himself."

Looking at the banged-up and bandaged

man, it certainly didn't seem like he should be trying to recuperate without some sort of full-time aid. With both legs like that, and one broken wrist, could he even make his way from the door to his bed? Izzy frowned. "What about Will?" she said, mentioning the friend who had been with him in Las Vegas the month before.

"He met with some trouble last night, too," Owen answered.

Her heart caught. *"What?"* Will had been the childhood summer love of her friend Emily, and it was the fault of the other couple, really, that she and Owen had said "I do" under the benevolent gaze of a very bad Elvis. "Is Will injured? Emily didn't tell me that when she called about you."

"Maybe she didn't want to worry you further," Owen said. "And he's going to be fine, but I'm not calling him to play nurse-maid."

"That settles it then," June Marston put in, her voice brisk. "You're coming home to your father and me."

Owen's jaw tightened. "No. Remember, you're going on that cruise in a couple of days with Caro and her fiancé."

"We'll cancel. This is more important." One of his mother's hands wrapped around the rails surrounding her son's bed, and the other gripped her husband's forearm. "A young man lost his life last night. It could have been you."

This time Izzy's heart stopped. It was all deathly quiet in her chest as she stared at

Owen. *A young man lost his life last night. It could have been you.*

Did that really happen? But the truth was there in Owen's face, in his eyes. Their summer-sky-blue went bleak and she couldn't believe that the man she'd laughed with and danced with and impulsively married could look so utterly sad.

His fingers, still entwined with hers, had gone cold. "Owen…" she whispered, as he closed his eyes. She didn't know if he was still aware she was in the room.

"Maybe I should go," she murmured as he continued to lie like a corpse—*God*—on the hospital bed.

"Yeah," he muttered. "Go away, Izzy. I've got enough to deal with right now."

It was permission to do what she wanted.

A reprieve, from his own mouth, in his own words. But his fingers were still entwined with hers and she stared at them, the sight turning her insides to mush as a sudden decision tumbled out of her mouth. "I'll take care of him at his place," she offered, directing her words to Owen's parents.

Something about the man made her impetuous, and she'd yet to understand why or get control of it. "That's what he wants," she heard herself continue, "and if that's what he wants, he'll be more comfortable there and also recuperate faster."

Instead of looking at her, June and Ross Marston were gazing on Owen. So she looked at him, too. His eyes were open again and he was staring at her. She didn't have a clue as to what he was thinking.

Though…was that a gleam of calculation in his eyes?

"What the hell are you saying, Izzy?" he asked.

She smiled, her extra-special charming one, because she figured she was going to need to be extra-special charming if she was going to help this man get back on his feet. The way she figured, her subconscious had come up with the idea as a way to atone for the sin of being such a craven coward five weeks before.

"I can rearrange my schedule to free up a few weeks. So I'm saying—" she told him, clasping his fingers in what she hoped was a reassuring grip "—I'm saying, 'Honey, I'm home,' for as long as you need me."

Chapter Two

Nice digs, Izzy thought, as she toured the middle level of Owen's condo while his brother settled him into the master bedroom upstairs. The bottom floor was a spacious garage. They'd parked Owen's SUV inside, but he hadn't allowed her to help maneuver him from the backseat where he'd been stretched out.

"Bryce can get me upstairs," he'd muttered, giving her a brief, hard look when she started to protest.

So he wasn't grateful to her, she acknowledged as she heard deep-voiced curses drift down the stairs. Or all that comfortable, either—with the pain from his injuries or her presence or perhaps both. But for her part, she thought she could be easy within the confines of his condo. There was a bedroom near his upstairs that he'd said she could use. She was used to making herself at home in strange hotel rooms, and Owen's abode—with its walls in contrasting shades of blue hung with groupings of framed, brightly colored primitive paintings—was several notches above any place she usually laid her head.

She ran her fingertips along the top of a manly yet soft-looking couch that had plump cushions and was set in front of an old trunk to serve as a coffee table. In the last five weeks when she'd thought of Owen, she'd never considered where and how he lived. Those few days they'd been together had been like a bubble in time. In her mind, after she'd left he'd still been in Las Vegas, standing in some casino somewhere like a slot machine with a better physique and all the flashy lights and tempting bells and whistles.

She crossed to a massive shelving unit built to surround a large-screen TV and that held DVDs, books and an interesting collection of firefighting memorabilia. Her finger slid along the rim of an old fireman's helmet.

"Where's the rest of your luggage?"

At the voice, she jumped and spun around, for a minute confusing the man coming into the room with the man she'd married. Their height was the same, and they had that same dark blond hair and square chin. But it was Bryce, not Owen, and she felt her tight stomach ease a little. She owed the man upstairs, and she hadn't been able to stop herself from offering to help him, but the idea of actually living with Owen did make her a bit nervous.

I can do this, though. I can dispense with the guilt I feel for running out on him by doing a good turn for the guy. She thought of the bandages, the cast, the cuts and bruises. *He needs me.*

"Where's the rest of your luggage?" Bryce asked again.

"I just have the one bag," she said, pointing to the small suitcase she'd set by the door. "I travel light."

Bryce's eyebrows rose. "I guess. I thought that was your makeup case."

Izzy shook her head. "I'm short. My feet are small. My clothes and shoes don't take up all that much room."

He was still looking at her one bag. "My brother, the lucky dog, marrying the only woman on planet Earth who can make do with less."

Make do with less? Izzy frowned. That wasn't how she saw herself. She was efficient. And capable of moving on in a moment— before she ever outstayed her welcome.

"So…you really are married to him?" Bryce asked.

"Well…" She sighed. "It's a long story."

"I don't need to be anywhere anytime soon." He crossed to the couch and sprawled onto the cushions.

"At the moment, I'd rather talk about Owen. How's he doing?" Izzy glanced up at the ceiling.

"Down for the count for a while, I'd guess. The meds and the trip home have done him in." He forked a hand through his hair. "I've been thinking. Maybe I should stay…."

"I thought you have a job more than an hour away in San Francisco."

He grimaced. "Yeah. The family biz. Granddad can't do it all by himself, though he wants to, and he and my dad are like oil and water. It's too far a commute, and in any case I would have trouble putting in my usual fourteen-hour days while taking care of Owen, too."

"But you see, I do have time." Then there was something else to consider—that chilling glimpse of Owen's desolate eyes that had scared her into volunteering for the gig as his personal home health aide. She was rebellious, yet not usually reckless, so it was still a surprise.

"And he seems willing to let you spend that time with him."

She held back a snort. "Only because it seemed the easiest way to put off your mother, I suspect."

Bryce laughed. "Yeah, I thought the same. She's a nice woman, really, but the prospect of having our mom hover could make a man desperate to settle for anyone else."

"Gee, thanks."

"Oops, sorry. It's not that you're not incredibly appealing in a chocolate-and-apricot-fairy kind of way—"

"Chocolate-and-apricot fairy?"

"Your hair. Your skin." He gestured to her and grinned. "Obviously, I'm the romantic brother in the family."

She'd thought marrying a woman after a three-days' acquaintance pretty darn romantic. Until she'd woken up the morning after the wedding and thought it was ridiculous and that both of them were certifiable. Owen had accused her of being a coward when he'd caught her checking out of the hotel, and she'd stalked off as if insulted— instead of showing her fear that he'd seen through her like no one else ever had.

"Why can't you imagine this might work?" he'd asked. She hadn't answered him, but she hadn't stuck around to end the marriage, either. Remembering the moment, her stomach jittered again with another attack of nerves and her gaze slid over to her one piece of luggage, conveniently resting beside the door. Maybe she should renege on her offer after all. Grab her little bag and get the heck out of town, just like she'd done in Las Vegas.

Leaving Owen behind again.

But this time hurt and needing…someone.

But he had family! Friends nearby! Roots in this town and also this nice home to call his own. She had none of those things, and she did just fine. Surely he would be okay—

"What happened?" she heard herself say, not taking her eyes off her suitcase, as if it were the governor's pardon that she could pick up if push came to shove. "I don't really know what happened the night of the fire."

She'd been avoiding finding out about it, too. Last evening she'd checked into one of those anonymous business hotels she was so familiar with—the ones that put a *USA TODAY* outside every door each morning, making it easy for her to avoid Paxton, California's, local headlines.

A glance at Bryce had her finding her way to an easy chair on the opposite side of the coffee table. She sank into it, eyeing him as he rubbed his face with his hands. "I don't like to think about it," he muttered.

Izzy had spent a lot of time alone as a child. Hence the interest in books. Hence the hyperactive imagination, and she realized that hers was cranking into over-drive without the benefit of facts to rein it in. She glanced with longing at her suitcase and the door just a few steps away. It would be so much easier…

"He and another guy were on top of a two-story house that was burning," Bryce said. "They were ventilating the roof. There was a collapse and Owen and the other man fell through—and through again, because fire had been eating at the guts of the place, too. They landed on the ground floor, banging up Owen. A beam also came down and…"

"And…?" she whispered.

"And crushed the other guy's chest. Jerry, his name was. Jerry Palmer."

Jerry Palmer. Izzy cursed her imagination, because she could picture a Jerry Palmer, see some man who was no longer in this world. And knowing the name made it so much more real about Owen, too—she could be a widow right now.

The man she'd married could have died.

Her gaze jumped to her suitcase again, but she dragged it away to focus on Owen's brother. "Bryce, I'm going to take care of him," she vowed. "I'm going to see him back on his feet. I promise."

He opened his mouth, but another voice sounded in the room. A little staticky, a lot grouchy. "What? You're going to leave me alone up here?"

"Intercom," Bryce explained, angling his head toward a device on the hallway wall that led to the kitchen.

"Oh." She rose at the same time as Bryce and saw him head toward the front door. "Wait. You're leaving already?"

"Is anyone there?" the surly voice sounded over the intercom again. "I'm bored. And starting to get cranky."

"'Starting'?" Izzy rolled her eyes and headed for the stairs, but then cast a last glance at Bryce, who already had his hand on the doorknob. "Words of wisdom, at least?"

"Just two." He gave her a bracing smile. "Good luck."

Owen breathed out a silent curse as the woman entered his bedroom, a tray in her hands. What had he been thinking to allow Isabella Cavaletti to play nurse to his patient? In a pair of jeans that clung to her petite but curvy frame, a V-necked T-shirt just hinting at those small breasts that had snuggled against his chest on the dance floor in Vegas, clearly she was going to cause new symptoms instead of helping to heal current injuries.

Just a breath of her fresh, sweet perfume and he was dizzy.

"Are you all right?" she asked, hurrying over to place the tray on his bedside table.

"I'm terrific," he said. No way was he going to let her know that her proximity made him woozy. He'd already spent way too much time at her mercy. Scowling, he admonished himself to hold tight to his righteous anger at her. "Five damn weeks, Izzy."

Hell. Had he said that out loud? It was all well and good to tell himself he was going to stay tough guy, but with those stupid meds in his system he was not in full control of himself. Five weeks. He hadn't meant to let her know he cared that much to keep count.

But for God's sake! Five damn weeks and not once had he heard from his wife.

She looked down, guilt stamped all over her face, so yeah, he'd definitely spoken his thoughts aloud. "I know how long it's been," she said, studying the carpet under her feet. "And I imagine you've spent the entire time trying to figure out the quickest, easiest way to undo what we did."

It took both people in the same place to do that, or at least knowing where both people were to do that. She could have been next door or in the Netherlands for all Owen had known. "More like I've been trying to figure out *why* we did what we did."

Without looking at him, she slid the tray from the bedside table and held it over his lap. "Scoot up a little bit. I made lunch."

Scooting up wasn't all the easy with three bum limbs, but he wasn't about to whine for help. And when she placed the food in front of him, he couldn't stop a half-smile from crossing his face. "You didn't forget."

She'd made him a grilled cheese sandwich that included sliced onions and tomato. His favorite. Sitting beside it was a glass of milk poured over ice.

"It wasn't that I had to remember. They're my favorite, too, right?"

"Right." That had been the craziest thing about those three days in Las Vegas. So much of it had felt so right. The way she fit against him, the way she liked her grilled cheese with onion and tomato, the way she took her milk over ice. But it was beyond preposterous to marry someone because their lunch choice mirrored your own. He'd realized that when she'd run away and not contacted him for five long weeks.

"I'll never hear an Elton John song and not remember—"

"Yeah." He shook his head. Somewhere into day two of their time together they'd made the mutual—and surreal—confession that they'd both misheard the chorus to the popular Elton John song "Tiny Dancer" as—

"Hold me closer, Tony Danza," she sang softly.

Owen winced. "Though it's nowhere close to being as dim as thinking Prince is singing 'Pay the rent, Collette,' in 'Little Red Corvette.'"

She frowned at him, her full lower lip pushing into a pout. He'd probably once considered that cute. "It wasn't me who thought Creedence Clearwater's song about a bad moon rising boasts that immortal line, 'There's a bathroom on the right.'"

Now he frowned. "It's a common mistake."

Even her snorts had a delicacy to them. "Says the guy who attended *way* too many fraternity beer bashes."

"Hey…" Well, there was a little truth in that, though how could she know? They hadn't spent time talking about their college years. He grimaced. "We're complete strangers to each other, aren't we?"

A flush rose up her neck and she looked away again. "Eat your lunch."

He picked up half the sandwich with his good hand. "What about you?"

"I'm not hungry."

She'd eaten like a bird those days in Las Vegas. And drank like a fish? But no, although they'd spent a fair amount of time in the bar at their hotel and also poolside with those froufrou, umbrella-topped drinks, he didn't think alcohol had played a major role in the tipsy feeling he'd felt in her company—and in the spur-of-the-moment decision they'd made to say "I do" to the strains of "Blue Suede Shoes."

"I blame Will and Emily," he muttered. "We were under the influence of their first-love vibes."

He heard a small, heartfelt sigh and shot Izzy a disgruntled look. That was the kind of thing that had gotten them into trouble five weeks ago. Those sweet little sighs, that soft look on her face, the dreamy expression in her eyes when she'd looked at her best friend, Emily, who had happened to run into Owen's best friend, Will, at the hotel. The other two had been childhood summer sweethearts and then lost touch after Will's parents had died, leaving him the sole support of his five brothers and sisters.

Their chance meeting had ended in Will and Emily making a date for drinks later, and they'd each dragged along their best friend. So there it was, Will and Emily, Owen and Izzy. They'd been witness to hours of amusing reminiscing, which included the long-ago vow the other two had once made to each other. "If only," Owen said now, "they'd not dreamed up that stupid promise to marry each other if they both weren't wed by thirty."

"Not so stupid now," Izzy said, perching on the end of the mattress, beyond where his feet were propped on pillows. "They're moving in together."

Owen looked over. "Huh?" Last he remembered, right before they'd been called out to the fire, Will had been wondering how two such smart single guys like themselves had somehow got themselves hitched.

"I talked to Emily last night. Apparently

what Will went through during the fire gave them both a clearer perspective on the promise they made in Las Vegas to love and cherish. They're a real couple now."

"Huh?" he said again. Will had come by his hospital room but had not a said a word about what he'd worked out with his wife. Maybe he hadn't wanted to rub it in. "Really?"

"She's packing boxes as we speak, and his ring is back on her finger."

Owen's gaze jumped from Izzy's face to her left hand. She'd had a ring, too. A simple gold circle that had come as part of the "Blue Suede and Gold Band" wedding package at the Elvis Luvs U Wedding Chapel. He remembered how her hand had trembled in his as he'd slid it down the short length of her slim finger. He remembered the tremulous smile on her lips and the glow in her eyes and how that dizziness he felt now he'd felt then, too, because she was so damn pretty and so…

His.

He'd liked the thought of that. He'd believed that what they'd had was real and could really work.

Before she'd left him and not bothered with a phone call or even an e-mail for thirty-seven days.

What was real was that he'd been an idiot. They'd both been idiots in that wedding chapel. "What the hell were we thinking?" he ground out again.

She shrugged, then studied the bed-spread beside her. "I'd been having a pretty stressful time at the librarians' convention. Not everyone is onboard with doing away with Dewey."

"Yeah. I remember having to pull you from a debate with a couple of crazies wearing T-shirts reading 'Melvil Now and Forever.'"

"Melvil Dewey." Izzy nodded. "Outside of Emily, I'd been a pariah for the five days before I met you. It was refreshing to have someone who looked at me with such, um…um…"

"Lust?" he provided helpfully.

She gave him that pouting frown again. "I was going to say approval."

His snort wasn't nearly as elegant as hers. "If that's what you want to call it, Izzy."

"Huh." She narrowed her eyes at him. "Now I know why Bryce says he's the romantic brother in the family."

Owen wondered just what the hell his brother was doing talking himself up to Owen's wife. "Was he *flirting* with you?"

"You don't have to look like it's such a shock."

"No. I—"

"He called me a chocolate-and-apricot fairy."

Chocolate-and-apricot fairy? Owen blinked. "My brother Bryce said that? He *was* flirting with you."

Izzy crossed her arms over her chest. "What? I don't strike you as a tasty fairy?"

No. He looked at her full mouth, the sparks in her brown eyes, the warm flush along her cheekbones. She struck him as…she just struck him. Right in the gut.

And then lower.

He curled his right hand into a fist to keep from reaching out for her. Even then, and even in the left hand that was casted, he could remember the texture of her soft, warm skin against his palms. He could remember sliding his hand down her neck and the thrum of her heartbeat against the pad of his thumb. His hands knew her, the sleek curve of her body from ribcage to hips, the dip at the small of her back, the resilient, round pillows of her behind when he urged her closer as they danced.

If he closed his eyes, he could feel her warm breath against his face.

He opened them, then jerked as he realized it really *was* her warm breath against his face. She was leaning over him to take away the tray. "You're sleepy," she said. "You need to rest."

With the view of her pretty breasts pushing against the clinging fabric of her shirt in his sight lines, he didn't think there was a chance in hell he'd be resting anytime soon. Sleep would be out of the question unless it was to dream about kissing her mouth, cupping those breasts and rubbing his thumbs over her nipples to bring them from soft blossom to tight buds.

In Las Vegas, she'd danced so close to him he'd felt the hard little berries brush against his shirt front and had barely stopped himself from hauling her, he-man style, over his shoulder and into his hotel room. After their marriage, though, she'd run off before they'd had a chance to share in any connubial bliss. No wonder she was still stirring up his libido, now that he was so close to her—and lying in a bed. Lucky he was temporarily incapacitated.

Though, hell, was he? What did a man need to make love? Not his ankle or his foot, anyway. And obviously, he thought, shifting on his mattress, the most relevant portion of him was working just fine.

Shifting again, he watched her walk toward the door with the tray. Did Izzy know about that cute little sway of her behind?

"Why did you offer to do this?" he suddenly asked. He knew why he'd taken her up on it. If he lost sight of her again, who knew how long it might be before he could track her down in order to end their farce of a marriage? And more, he wanted a chance to dissect exactly why they'd followed Will and Emily's crazy idea and gotten married five minutes after their friends. He hoped that by breaking down that decision, the attraction he'd felt for the woman wouldn't have a chance to ever come together again.

She shrugged. "Would you accept it seemed like a good idea at the time?"

Like his notion that bringing her into his everyday life would prove there was nothing left of the attraction he'd felt for her in the land of lust and lost wages, he thought. They said whatever happened in Vegas was supposed to stay in Vegas, after all.

His gaze tracked the sensual roll of her hips as she kept on walking, and the sexiness of it gave another undeniable tug to his libido. Which just went to prove there was no damn truth in advertising.

Chapter Three

Owen ignored his mother's long-suffering sigh and watched Izzy enter the master bedroom carrying yet another tray—this one bearing two glasses of white wine for the women and two bottles of handcrafted beer for Owen and his dad. He hadn't taken any meds since yesterday, so Owen figured he could enjoy a good brew.

His mom shot him a disgruntled look and turned her attention to the younger woman. "Isabella," she said, "your new husband's being very close-mouthed about your wedding. Please tell me a detail or two."

"Well…" Izzy bent to put the tray onto the narrow coffee table in the room's sitting area.

There was a couch, an easy chair that he was sitting on and an ottoman that was being used to prop up his lower legs, as well as a second matching chair, all gathered around a fireplace. Owen's dad had busied himself setting a small fire inside it when he'd first arrived. Now that he'd helped Owen in and out of a shower—thank you, plastic stool and a waterproof covering for his cast—his father kneeled to light the kindling and logs. As the autumn dusk settled outside, the reflection of the flames provided a camouflage for the blush Owen suspected was warming Izzy's cheeks.

"Our wedding?" Izzy repeated. "I, um…"

June Marston took the wineglass the younger woman handed over and returned an easy smile. "At least tell me about your dress."

Izzy shot Owen a look. Oh, yeah. Her dress. While like every other man he knew he wasn't particularly style-conscious, no way could he forget that dress. Strapless. Spangled. Low cut in the cleavage area. High cut in the leg area.

And fire-engine red.

In Vegas you could rent just about anything, and he'd shelled out a couple of twenties for ten minutes with a poof of white stuff that she'd pinned in her hair as a veil and a bouquet of white roses she'd held in her hand while they repeated their vows. He remembered thinking she looked as sweet and spicy as peppermint candy, and his mouth had watered in anticipation of sampling her flavor.

"My dress, uh…" The next look she shot him snapped him out of his happy little reverie. *Get me out of this,* it said.

He supposed she didn't want to tell his mother she'd married him wearing a barely there dress and a pair of scarlet, spike-toed high heels that had made him swallow, hard, so he wouldn't let out his groan of lust—or "approval," as some others liked to term it.

Owen cleared his throat. "Mom, that

reminds me. Izzy wants *you* to tell *her* something. She was asking about what I was like as a kid, and I thought you'd be the best source for that."

Izzy latched onto the idea in a way that would have been flattering if he hadn't known she just wanted to avoid the subject of their impromptu wedding. "I'd love to hear everything you can tell me about him."

Owen glanced at his father, now seated beside his mother on the couch. The older man wore a half-smile and sported an amused glint in his eyes. *Nice dodge,* he mouthed to Owen.

You could fool some of the parents some of the time....

And this time he'd succeeded in veering his mother onto a different track. He relaxed with his beer, letting her talk of his Little League years, then seasons of peewee football, followed by details of his high school endeavors.

"Salutatorian," his mother told Izzy. "He graduated second in his high school class. From there he went on to college where he was an economics major, heading for an MBA degree. Which I always considered a very useful field of study."

"Unlike how I'm employed today," Owen couldn't help put in, "because doing things like, I don't know, saving property is just so…irrelevant."

His mother frowned. "You know I didn't mean it like that."

She probably didn't, but he still had a sharp chip on his shoulder left over from the discussions he'd had with his parents and grandfather years ago when he decided against a master's degree and for a place in the fire academy instead. He watched Izzy rise from her chair to perch on the arm of his.

"Not only property," she said, touching his shoulder. "You save lives, too."

But not Jerry Palmer. That knowledge rushed in on Owen in a sudden, cold wave. Nausea churned his stomach and he felt clammy again.

"Owen?" His father was looking at him with concern. "Are you all right, son?"

Glancing around their small circle, he could see identical expressions on the faces of Izzy and his mom. "I'm fine," he said, forcing a half-laugh into his voice. "Well, except for the fact that I'll have to put off beating you at golf again for a few weeks, Dad. Though by the time you get back from your cruise I should be up to it."

When the other three continued to study him with narrowed eyes, he lifted his hands, even the casted one, and pasted on what he hoped was a grin. "What's there to be upset about? I have an unexpected vacation, a fire in the fireplace, the company of a beautiful woman and my loving family."

Maybe his grin worked. His mother gave a little nod and then turned to Izzy again. "Speaking of family…I'd like to hear all about yours, too."

"What can I say?" Izzy's smile looked as effortless as his had been difficult.

What could she say? It occurred to Owen that she'd never said. Not in Vegas—where admittedly they'd been living in a moment that had little room for family histories— and not in the three days she'd been in this house with him, though he'd been sleeping a lot as he tapered off the pain meds.

He slanted a glance at her now, happy to keep the conversation steered away from himself and how he was feeling. Guilty. Queasy. Damn downcast. None of these made for good conversation.

"Izzy?" he prompted when she still didn't speak.

She shrugged, that smile still curving her mouth. "I'm Italian."

"Yes," his mother said. "And your mother and father—"

"I have the pair of them," Izzy confirmed. "Can I get anyone more to drink?" She made to rise.

Owen placed the weight of his cast over her thigh to hold her down. "You wait on me too much as it is," he said. "People can help themselves."

"That's the point of me being here, Owen," she answered. "To take care of you."

"A wife doesn't consider taking care of her husband a burden," his mother said. "And a husband would feel exactly the same way. Wouldn't you be there for Isabella if she was stuck in bed, Owen?"

He looked up into Izzy's face and the answer to his mother's question struck him with full force. No matter how mad he was that she'd left him, if Izzy was stuck in bed, if she couldn't get away from him like she'd done in Las Vegas, he'd use the opportunity to do more than make her meals or bring her the remote control. If she were on that bed over there, he'd be doing his damnedest to seduce her into letting him have more of those sweet kisses they'd once exchanged. He'd be exerting all his influence to let her let him undo those little buttons marching down the front of her shirt until he could look his fill at her pretty breasts.

Yeah, some things didn't stay in Vegas. Like lust.

Her thigh hardened under his touch and he heard the little catch in her breath. Her tongue reached out to make a nervous flick along the fullness of her bottom lip.

He'd want to do that, too.

"I'd like to give them a call," his mother was saying.

Izzy's eyes went wide and her gaze shifted from his face to the older woman on the couch. "What?" she said.

"If you'd give me their number, I'd like to phone them and introduce myself as your new mother-in-law. Maybe they're available to come for a visit soon so we can all get acquainted."

"Oh…well…" Her thigh started jumping as her knee bounced in a jittery movement. "That's not, um…"

Not a good idea? He supposed she'd kept the news of their wedding as secret as he had. And while he could mention that to his mother, and then flat-out inform his parents that this marriage was a temporary situation just waiting for a permanent solution, he…well, he didn't feel like it. Because…

Because his mother might take the truth as a reason to apply the screws and get him out of his place and into the penthouse in San Francisco. He didn't want that.

Because stating the bald-faced truth about their marriage to his family would surely banish Izzy from his life. And he didn't want that, either. Not now. Not yet. Not when he supposed they had forms to fill out and papers to sign.

He stroked his fingertips over Izzy's nervous leg. "Mom, we don't want visitors right now."

"But—"

"Think about it, Mom. This is really my and Izzy's honeymoon."

Izzy's leg stilled. Her gaze jumped to his. The fire's flames reflected warmly on her apricot skin—damn Bryce, he was never going to get that fairy comment out of his head—but there was another flush warming her skin, as well.

Embarrassment, or that "approval"?

It didn't matter, not when just looking at her could have him remembering past the need to end their marriage, remembering beyond the argument in the Vegas hotel lobby, remembering back to that incredible, undeniable physical attraction he'd experienced the moment they'd met. It overrode every sensible thought, every angry response to what she'd done.

Izzy licked her bottom lip again. His fingers tightened on her thigh.

Owen's dad cleared his throat. "June, I think that's our cue to head on home. We still have some packing to finish up, if I'm not mistaken."

Owen knew it wasn't smart to be feeling this, but he couldn't seem to extinguish the rising heat. Catching Izzy's hand, he brought her fingers to his mouth. "Good idea, Dad," he said, brushing his lips against her knuckles.

That small hitch in her breath reached Owen's ears, and that little sound seemed to reach lower, too, where his body demonstrated so very clearly that not every part of it was broken.

"I'll...I'll just show your parents out," Izzy said, her gaze locked on his.

Owen squeezed her fingers. Attraction,

not good sense, ran the show right now. And it didn't want her moving an inch from him. It wanted her close, and hell, Izzy *was* still his wife. "You stay right here, baby. They know the way."

Owen's parents were rising to leave and Izzy really felt as if she should accompany them to the front door, but she found herself pulled down into Owen's lap instead. "What—"

"Play along," he murmured as he nuzzled her hair. "Or else they'll linger and we'll end up confessing one of our wedding guests was a pretend Priscilla Presley."

She squirmed, because she was ticklish right behind her ear and his breath was so hot and his—well, something hard was pressing against her bottom.

"Bye, Mom, Dad. Have a great trip," Owen called out. His voice sounded hoarse and she told herself it was from smoke, not sexual promise. "Be sure not to write. Don't phone."

"Owen," Izzy started to protest, but he put his mouth over hers, cutting off her words. Reminding her of what it was like to kiss him.

Good. Kissing Owen was good. His uninjured hand cupped her cheek and kept her mouth turned to his. His tongue painted the seam between her lips and it was as if she didn't have a will of her own. She opened for him, and even reached out her wet tongue to his.

At the touch, a sizzle shot through her system, a jagged, hot sensation that had her gasping for breath. Her mouth jerked away. She swallowed, her eyes staring into his.

They were so close she could see that the edges of the cut at the bridge of his nose were drawing together. He could have died, she thought again. Owen could have died.

His hand shifted from her face to curl around the back of her head. As he speared his fingers through her hair, he brought her mouth close to his again. Close enough to brush his lightly, setting off more sparklers.

"Owen," she said, though she didn't know why saying his name gave her such satisfaction.

"Shh," he murmured. "Make this look good. They may tiptoe back up the stairs, and we want to look like real honeymooners, don't you think?"

Right. She wasn't sure why she was agreeing, but it didn't really matter when it was just like Las Vegas again, with the incredible feelings she experienced in his arms welling up, buoying her on a combined tide of mental well-being and physical excitement.

Izzy stroked her hands over his thick hair and she heard him groan as she opened her mouth and took his tongue inside again. Heat blossomed over her skin, and she pressed closer to him, even though she knew more closeness wasn't going to cool her down.

The sound of a distant door slamming stilled them both. "Hey, bro!" Bryce's voice. Steady footsteps said he was coming up the stairs.

Izzy jumped and made to move off Owen's lap, but he held her there. "This is embarrassing," she told him.

"It will be more embarrassing—at least

for me—if you get up right now, honey." He stroked a hand over her hip and she felt her face heat up again as she realized her body was covering up what had happened to his.

"But I'm too heavy."

He half groaned, half laughed. "Believe me, that's not what I'm complaining about right now."

Bryce bounded into the bedroom, grinning and appearing not the least put out by finding his brother and Izzy snuggled up on a single chair. "What's up?"

Owen slanted her a glance, one eyebrow winging high. "Want to answer that one?"

Bad. Bad boy. She sent the message with a quelling glance—they taught a course on it in librarian school—then tried to appear casual and not at all a little uncomfortable in her current position. "We just had a visit from your parents."

"And now you," Owen said. "Bryce, it's at least an hour to here from your office. Why the hell have you come?"

"Is that any way to greet your loving little brother?"

"Well, yeah, considering I have a life and that you should get one outside of your assistant, your financial reports and your refereeing between Granddad and Dad. If you're taking off early it should be to visit a woman."

"Who says I'm not?" Bryce smiled again, one hundred bright watts of masculine appeal that he shot straight at Izzy. "How's my beautiful fairy today?"

Her heart rocked a little under all the male allure, but probably because his ultrasexy big brother had already set the thing tumbling with that string of surprise kisses. "I'm—"

"Completely immune to your dubious charms," Owen finished for her. Then he frowned as Bryce picked up his beer bottle and drained the half-filled bottle dry. "Hey! That's mine."

"You know I always want whatever you have," he said, sliding his teasing glance toward Izzy's face again. "If I can't play with your wife—"

"Which you can't."

"—then sheesh, don't begrudge me some of your beverage."

Owen was shaking his head, and though Izzy suspected he was amused by his brother's antics, he had his casted arm secured against her middle. With his other hand, he adjusted her a little so that her head fit under his chin. She felt him press his lips on the top of her hair.

Bryce was beaming at them both. "I do like to see you so happy, bro."

She would have craned her neck to look at Owen, but he had her clamped too closely to him. Did he appear happy? She wondered, because over the past few days, more than once she'd caught him looking very much less than that. Moody and brooding described it better, as if there were a dark cloud hanging over his head that was poised to drench him in a downpour.

She was pretty sure he wasn't sleeping well. But when she'd asked him about it, he'd made clear that his nighttime habits were off-limits.

"Happy?" Owen stiffened, then patted her hip in a dismissive gesture. "Yeah, well. Could you move, Iz? My legs are going numb."

Of course Izzy did as directed, and it gave her an opportunity to check out that "happy" herself—and realize it wasn't the way she'd characterize his expression. Not at all. A minute ago he'd been exchanging passionate kisses with her, but now he looked as if he'd much rather be alone. His gaze was remote, his eyes focused on something she couldn't see.

She found herself dropping to the arm of his chair like before, then flicking a glance in Bryce's direction.

He looked worried now, too. "Did I say something wrong?"

"I don't know what you're talking about," Owen replied, his gaze still on that faraway place.

"It just seemed to get a little, I don't know, chilly in here." Bryce frowned, studying his brother.

"Stoke the fire, then."

With a shrug, Bryce ambled over to the brass log carrier set on the hearth. There was some newspaper wedged behind the stacked logs, and he pulled it out. "Wait a second. You don't mean to burn today's copy of the *Paxton Record* here, do you? It doesn't look as if you've read it."

Owen made a dismissive gesture. "I don't want to."

"Mr. News Junkie turning down info? I know it's just the local rag, but you're as addicted to that as your daily dose of those big-city papers you read online."

Bryce was holding it out, but it was Izzy who took the sheets from him. She remembered bringing it in this morning, but she'd just tucked it on Owen's breakfast tray and not given it a second thought.

Now that she saw the odd stiffness in his body, though, she looked down at the paper with suspicion. Above the fold, a photo of a fireman in full gear. *Jerry Palmer,* the caption read. The top story was coverage of his funeral, which had taken place the day before.

Her stomach folded in on itself. Oh, no. "Owen. I wish someone had let us know about the service…"

His face gave nothing away. "I knew about it. The captain called."

"We could have found a way to go—"

"It's okay." He was shaking his head. "Everyone understands."

She didn't understand. Why hadn't he mentioned it? Was it because he didn't want to be seen by his friends and colleagues beat up and battered, or was there something else turning in this man's head?

Bryce didn't seem to be any more enlightened than Izzy. Though he'd finished building up the fire, he still stood by the hearth, gazing on his brother's face, a line between his eyebrows. "Bro…"

Owen curled a hand around Izzy's waist and pulled her into his lap again. Then he bent his head to place a hot kiss against the side of her neck. She shivered, half because it felt so good and half because she knew he was using the move as a way to dodge Bryce's scrutiny.

"Be a bro back and get out of here, will you?" Owen asked.

Bryce didn't appear ready to be dismissed, though. He crossed to the couch and dropped onto the cushions, stretching out his long legs. "Like you said, it took me over an hour to get here from the office. You're not going to kick me out after less than fifteen minutes, are you?"

Owen took Izzy's face in his good hand and turned her lips to his. The kiss he gave her was chaste compared to some they'd shared, but she felt her tight stomach start to unfurl again, even knowing he had something else on his mind besides a renewed acquaintance with her mouth.

Owen's lips lifted. "You don't mind being a third wheel, Bryce?"

"I mind being BS'd," his brother replied. "Is something bothering you, Owen?"

"Yeah, I can't kiss my woman without you looking on."

"Really, Owen," Bryce answered, his eyes narrowing. "Is something biting your butt about what happened that night?"

"What night? Last night?" He laid another soft kiss on Izzy's bottom lip. "Last night when I was alone with my wife?" He caressed her shoulder with his hand.

The same hand that he'd used last night to morosely flip the channels on the TV remote, rarely responding to her in anything other than grunts. She might as well have been a doorknob for all the attention he'd paid to her. The day hadn't been so bad, but as the night descended, as it was doing now, his mood seemed to go down with it.

"I'm talking about the night of your… accident," Bryce clarified. Then his voice quieted, all his earlier humor gone. "Are the memories of it bothering you?"

Owen appeared to swallow his impatience. "Look. I'm good. The fact is, I don't even remember much, okay? I remember studying for a class Will and I are taking on haz mats, I remember the alarm, but after that it's all sorta smoky." He put on a grin that Izzy would swear was forced and shifted his gaze her way. "Hey, librarian, I punned."

"You did." She shot a look at Bryce, then turned back to Owen, not knowing what to think.

"I get a prize, don't I?" And he swooped in

to take it, laying a dramatic kiss on her mouth. Another show, but she went along with it anyway. Fine. It was hard to turn down a kiss that potent.

"Okay, okay," Bryce said as they came up for air. "I get the hint. You two lovebirds want to be alone."

"Thanks for coming." Owen settled back into the cushions of his chair. "Next time, call first."

"Yeah, yeah," the younger man grumbled, waving a hand over his shoulder.

Then he was gone, leaving Owen and Izzy alone. She looked at him, but he was looking at the flames now roaring in the fireplace. A log popped, and Owen jolted, as if a ghost had jumped out and yelled "Boo!"

"You're faking," she heard herself say. God, he *was* faking.

His gaze jumped to hers. "What?" he demanded.

She focused on his face, taking in that bleak expression once more in his eyes. "You're faking. You faked to your family that our marriage is real. You faked to your parents that we're having ourselves a 'honeymoon.' And now you're faking that you're feeling any kind of 'good' about what had happened the night of that fire."

His eyes had narrowed to slits. His uncasted hand was curled into a tense fist. "It's none of your damn business, Izzy."

"Owen—"

"Why don't you just move to a hotel? From there you can figure out what we need to do about this marriage, then we'll sign the damn papers."

"Your signing hand is in a cast," she pointed out.

And it wasn't just his body that was damaged. She knew now that something deeper was hurt, as well. And Izzy Cavaletti owed this man her help until he healed—all the way. "So I'm sticking," she told him.

Of course, he didn't look very happy about it.

She raised her brows. "Think about it, my friend. Do you want your parents and Bryce here hovering? Or just me?"

She had him there. She knew it.

Except he was looking angry again, instead of grateful, and there was no sign of the man who had kissed her silly just a few minutes before. "Fine," he finally ground out. "Stay. But if you're not in my bed,

Isabella Cavaletti, then you stay the hell out of my head!"

Since sharing his bed was about the worst idea she could think of, Izzy welcomed the distinctive ring of her cell phone—"Bohemian Rhapsody"—and hurried away to answer it. Her retreat gave Owen the last word, but that seemed the safest course.

Chapter Four

College football played on Owen's big-screen TV. He was lying on his bed, pretending to be immersed in each play, when all he saw were figures of blue and red scrambling on a green field. He made himself blink every once in a while to keep the colors in focus, but he let the rest of his consciousness drift, thinking about nothing, willing himself into a comfortable catatonic state.

Izzy moved into the periphery of his vision and he drew his eyebrows together, as if the success of the defensive line was tantamount to victory for the free world—or at least as if he had some cash riding on the game. Anything to get Izzy to go away and leave him alone.

"Look who's here," she called out brightly, waving a hand. "And they brought lunch."

Owen slid his gaze in her direction. Damn, there was a "who" all right, two of them, and they were beaming smiles and bearing bags. He felt obliged to smile at them, because at least they'd serve as a temporary buffer between Owen and all the things he didn't want to think about. "Will," he said, greeting his best friend and colleague at the Paxton F.D. "And Emily. It's nice to see you again."

The last time he'd seen the smiling woman had been in Vegas, as matron of honor to Izzy, his bride.

Will gripped his right hand, giving it a strong squeeze. "You said you were doing well on the phone, but Emily said she had to see you in person."

Emily frowned and shoved her husband aside to kiss Owen on the cheek. "It was all his idea," she whispered. "Not that I didn't want to see you myself, but apparently he feels it necessary to hide behind me in order to preserve his macho image."

Owen could certainly understand that.

Right now he was all about preserving his macho image, which wasn't easy when a man was laid up, with a lousy memory and a temporary wife he was forced to depend on for his every mouthful. Except this time Will and Emily had brought a meal. "What's in the bags?" he asked, glancing at Will.

His friend was finishing rearranging the furniture in the living area of the master bedroom suite so that Owen could remain propped on the bed yet still be part of the group when they settled onto the sofa and chairs. "Subs from Louie's," he said, and grabbed up the remote on the bedside table to thumb off the TV.

"Hey!" Owen said. "I'm into the game."

Will blinked at him. "You never watch college football."

"It's a new habit." A new habit that was better than watching his wife and *much* better than talking to her. No, it wasn't that he didn't want to talk to Izzy. At the moment, he didn't much want to talk to anyone. He took a big bite of the salami-and-cheese sandwich Emily handed to him on a paper plate. "Put it back on, Will."

With a shrug, his friend complied, but he muted the sound. Owen frowned, but what could he do? He supposed he could take fifteen or so minutes of innocuous conversation.

"So are you all moved into Will's?" Izzy asked Emily.

She nodded and started chattering about painting a bathroom. Owen tuned out, then realized that his best friend was staring at

him again. "What now?" He grabbed up a
napkin and wiped his chin. "Mustard?"

"I'm just waiting for the 'I told you so.'"
Will glanced over at the two women, who
were immersed in their own conversation.

"Huh?"

Will chewed a bite of his own sandwich.
"The last time we really talked was on the
night of the fire."

The night that was only that smoky memory
to Owen, and hadn't he established that he
liked it that way? "Busy time," he mumbled.

"We were studying for the haz-mat course
we're enrolled in. I was bemoaning my
married state and wondered aloud how two
such smart guys as ourselves could have
gotten hitched in Vegas. You know, that big
mistake of ours."

"Huh," Owen grunted. He remembered also vowing that he was going to track down Izzy after that very shift ended. Goes to show he should have been more careful about what he wished for. He should have been specific that tracking her down didn't include taking her into his home.

Okay, fine, he'd agreed to letting her stay here. But he hadn't realized how pretty she would look in the morning, and how sexy she'd look at noon and how good she'd smell at night, straight from the shower. And he hadn't considered how talkative she would be, too. She was a librarian, for God's sake! He expected more of her nose in a book and less of her nose in his life.

She'd casually asked him a couple of

questions about the fire. The name Jerry Palmer had passed her lips a time or two.

He didn't want to talk about the fire or Jerry.

"You asked me," Will said, breaking into his thoughts, "if I was so sure that what we'd done in Vegas was a mistake."

"Of course it was a mistake," Owen blurted out. Then he realized the women had gone quiet and that both of them were looking at him. Great. He'd just insulted his best friend and his best friend's wife. Not to mention the woman he'd married, too.

"I mean…I mean…" He shoved his plate off his lap. Hell. "No offense meant, okay?"

Will calmly took another bite of his sandwich. "Best damn mistake of my whole life." Reaching over, he ruffled the ends of Emily's hair. She beamed back sexy sunshine that softened her husband's face.

Izzy was the one sending him a dirty look. Her usually warm brown eyes were cooling, and that plump bottom lip of hers was pushed out in disapproval. "I'm sure the newlyweds appreciate your best wishes."

He swallowed his groan. "Look—"

Emily hopped up, interrupting his apology. "I brought chocolate chip cookies, too. C'mon, Iz, help me get them." She dragged her friend up by the elbow.

As the women left the room, taking the remains of the sandwiches and plates, Will grinned at Owen. "That's right. She said chocolate chip cookies. My wife bakes."

Wife. "But…but…" Regardless of what he'd expressed on the night of the fire, could this really be his best friend's happy ending? "Are you absolutely sure you want to be a married man?"

That, after all, had been the opposite of what Will wanted for himself as they'd headed for Vegas going on six weeks ago. Finally freed of the responsibilities of raising five younger siblings, Will had professed to be ready to take up the reins of a wild bachelorhood.

Will propped his feet on the nearby ottoman. "I *want* to be married to Emily."

And she was already living with Will, just as Izzy was living with Owen. Didn't Will find all the female companionship distracting? The soft patter of their footsteps, the heady smell of their perfume, the way they looked in jeans, or a robe or even a towel turban? But then, Will got to work out his distraction between the sheets, while Owen had to ignore his by watching college football on TV or pretending to take another dozenth nap.

"You okay, Owen?"

"Huh," he grunted again, and grabbed up the remote to thumb up the sound on his set. More little insects scrambled across the green screen. Go…whichever team was losing. He was identifying with the underdog these days, big time.

"How're things with you and Izzy?"

"I don't want to talk about it." Remember, he didn't want to talk about anything! Why else did Will think he had the volume up loud enough to hear the announcers drone on about their glory days throwing the pigskin around? Good God, was there no one more self-involved than a sports announcer with a pretty face and a half-dozen seasons in the NFL?

"What about the night of the fire? The night that Jerry died and we were hurt?" Will asked.

We were hurt. Oh, crap. Yeah, there was someone more self-involved than those bull-necked bobbleheads on TV. And that would be him. Will had been injured that night, too—he'd gone through his own harrowing experience. "Are *you* okay?"

"Twisted ankle, already all healed up. Nothing close to what you're dealing with." He looked at his feet, propped on the ottoman, then he looked back over at Owen. "The worst part was when I was trapped under that metal awning. I had a few bad moments wondering if I was going to be crushed under the metal or cooked like stew over a camp stove. Put a few things in perspective for me. My brothers and sisters. Emily."

"Yeah," Owen replied. He had bad moments, too, recalling that hazy night. What had he done wrong? How had he let Jerry down? Surely there was something…

"Tell me, Will," he said gruffly. He couldn't retreat to the land of silence any longer. There was no way he could duck the thoughts in his head. "Tell me about that night."

Will frowned. "You remember."

"I can't…" Owen rubbed a hand over his hair, wishing he could still put off the truth forever. "I don't have the details straight. But I must have made an error in judgment."

"No." Will's adamant voice came clearly through the bedroom doorway, halting Izzy in her trip back to the bedroom with Emily and the cookies. "It wasn't you, Owen. You didn't do anything wrong. That damn fire was responsible for Jerry's death."

Izzy's heart flopped in her chest. Oh, no. Oh, God. This is what she'd been worrying about. She shifted closer to hear better, then felt her friend yank her back by the arm. "Downstairs and to the kitchen for us," she whispered.

"But…" But then she let her words subside. Owen would have clammed up if she and Emily returned, and it was important that he get out whatever he was bottling up inside him. His emotions definitely needed a release.

And she could use the respite from her own. A little chat with her best friend should be the soothing balm she needed.

The two women retreated to the kitchen, and Izzy set down the tray on the counter. "Shall I make some tea?" she asked her friend.

Emily smiled. "Really? You? Tea? Quite the domestic goddess you've turned out to be."

"You should see what I can do with those little coffeemakers that come in hotel rooms. Three-course meals—though all with the distinctive seasoning of Sanka."

"Ew." Emily leaned against the countertop as Izzy bustled around the kitchen. "So, what's new besides your new stint as 'Isabella Cavaletti, Home Nurse?'"

Izzy gave a little shrug. "Not much. I heard that my *Zia* Sophia passed away."

"Oh, Iz…"

She shrugged again. "She was ninety-seven when she died. I lived with her in third grade—so, twenty years ago? Funny lady. She made a mean ziti and never rose before noon."

Emily frowned. "Never rose before noon? Who got you up for school? Made your breakfast?"

"The saintly three of me, myself and I." She caught the look of sympathy in Emily's gaze. "Girlfriend, it wasn't Dickens. There were clean, folded clothes in the drawers and Pop-Tarts in the kitchen cupboard."

"Still…"

"A mean ziti can overcome many nutritional challenges." The kettle was starting to whistle, so Izzy hurried to the stovetop.

"Do you need some time away from Owen to attend the funeral? I'm sure Owen's brother would help out, since his parents and sister are on that cruise. If not, Will or I—"

"Oh, no." Izzy waved off the offer. "*Zia* was laid to rest about four months ago. I only heard because I made a call to one of my cousins last week. I was concerned because my mother's number hasn't been working."

"*Izzy.*" Emily took a breath, seeming to get a hold of herself. "All right, the homicidal urge over the way your family forgets about you is passing. Wait—did you say your mother's number wasn't working? Is *she* all right?"

"Yes. She's on a trip, packing for a trip, un-packing for a trip, planning her next trip. One of those." Her parents had led tours throughout Europe for the past thirty years. "She got a new phone and a new number for reasons not quite clear to me in the fifteen seconds we had to talk before her flight was called."

"And your father?"

"He was reading a newspaper, but apparently gave a pinkie-wave when he heard it was me on the phone."

Emily heaved a sigh. "They're not—"

"Anything different than they've ever been. It's when you start expecting more that you get disappointed by people."

"Some people *won't* disappoint you, Iz. Some people will be there always and—"

Izzy shut her up with a brief, hard hug. "Sure. Like Will is there for you, Emily."

Emily's eyes narrowed. "Is there some other family thing you should be telling me about?"

"No! You already know all about my family 'things.'" And the last thing that would relax her was a rehash of her relatives. "So, spill all about marital bliss."

"You're married, too, Izzy."

"And I'm going to have to do something about that, I realize. Did you get very far in finding out what it takes to annul—" She broke off at the odd expression crossing her friend's face. "Let's not talk annulments then. Let's talk happy husbands and winsome wives."

"'Winsome'?" The word made Emily

grimace. "What the heck are you talking about, Isabella?"

"I don't know." She laughed. "I know nothing about how this coupledom thing is supposed to work."

"Is that how you see you and Owen? Are you a couple now?"

"No. That wedding thing was impulsive, spontaneous, and we place the blame entirely on you and Will."

"Hey, we didn't force that ring on your finger."

Izzy smiled a little at the memory of Owen beside her, the flash of his smile and that wild—and absurdly right—feeling she'd had as he slid the narrow band down her left ring finger. Common sense hadn't kicked in until the next morning, when he'd caught her in the lobby, trying to sneak out of the hotel. She'd been in the checkout line, tugging on that matrimonial symbol. "Did you know window cleaner is the best method to remove a ring?"

"I'll put that in my reference librarian files," Emily said, rubbing her thumb over her own wedding band. "Though I'm planning to keep this one on forever."

"I believe it."

Emily frowned a little. "Owen didn't seem to."

"It's just that he's in a cantankerous frame of mind," Izzy answered. "He's been pretty much set on moody since the day we walked in here."

"Will thinks he's upset about Jerry."

"Me, too," Izzy admitted. "And maybe

beyond the grief that you would expect. But I don't know what to do about it."

"Chicken soup sans Sanka flavoring?"

"That's the best I have to offer so far." Though her mind drifted to those kisses they'd shared since she'd moved in. Granted, they'd been more for show than for seduction, but the sparks had been there all the same. Their Las Vegas experience had been similar. An instant, fiery attraction that at the time had seemed serendipitous and delightful. The sensation of his arms around hers had been just like the books said, a "coming home" sort of feeling that even someone who'd never had a real home could recognize.

On the dance floor, she'd fit her cheek in that hollow where his shoulder met his chest and she'd be as comfortable as if he were her pillow, but also tingly and twitchy at the same time. Her skin had shivered at his slightest touch, and when he kissed that sensitive corner of her jaw, her knees had gone soft.

"Izzy. Izzy!"

She blinked, coming down to earth as Emily sharply called her name. "What? What?"

"Our heroes are calling for dessert," she said. "Where were you?"

"Oh." She put the teapot on the tray, added mugs, made room for a cold jug of water and two glasses. "Here and there. You know me. The proverbial rolling stone."

They climbed the stairs, but reaching the landing, Izzy transferred the tray to her friend. "I forgot napkins. Take this in and I'll be back in a jiff."

It was slightly more than that because she had to find a new package and then practically gnaw her way into the shrink-wrapped plastic to get to the rainbow of folded paper. She clutched a handful as she approached the doorway of the large master suite.

The sight there made her pause. Emily sat in Will's lap, just as she'd sat on Owen's a few nights before. Will's arm was curled about his wife's waist in a gesture that was protective and possessive. They both wore playful expressions and were feeding each other cookies as if they were pieces of wedding cake.

The tenderness of the moment had Izzy's

heart flip flopping uncomfortably in her chest again, as if someone were turning a pancake. She'd grown up in a number of households during her childhood, and though most were those of aging female relatives, a time or two she'd been in a home led by a married couple. The husband-and-wife teams had always fascinated her. They were Italian households, so there were often a lot of loud voices and chaos in the kitchen, but the few times she'd witnessed a moment like this between a man and a woman it had skewered her heart.

Because she didn't know how to make that happen for herself. When she'd seen it, she'd tried memorizing the moves and deciphering the dynamics, but she'd been aware that her background was too full of

Zia Sophias and solo Pop-Tart breakfasts to comprehend the ins and outs of the couple thing.

Still, it was pretty to look at.

Her gaze drifted toward Owen. He was apparently immune to the sweet domestic drama playing out just a few feet away from him. His attention was focused on the football game on the screen, and he didn't look as if his discussion with Will—*I must have made an error in judgment*—had offered him any ease. His expression was stony and when he shifted on the bed, he winced.

Her heart rocked again and she had to force herself to stride into the room, wearing a smile. "Hey," she said. "It's time for your pain relievers, Owen."

He didn't look away from the game. "I don't need anything." His voice was surly.

"Except a mood transplant, maybe," she murmured, dropping the napkins by the lovebirds and heading for the bedside table where the big bottle of ibuprofen sat.

"I heard that," he said, still not looking at her.

"Oops." She made a big play of putting her hand over her mouth. "Did I say something I shouldn't have?"

His mouth twitched, then his eyes shifted her way. Their startling blue slammed into her, and it was she who rocked this time, her whole body, rolling back on her heels as she saw the spark of amusement catching fire in his gaze. "Okay, I'm being inhospitable, as well as cranky, and you're an angel to put up with me."

She took in a careful breath to give herself time to camouflage the way that reluctant, self-deprecating humor affected her. It was as good as a spin on a Las Vegas dance floor. Her head felt just as dizzy.

For the next half hour, he applied himself to being a more genial host. He turned off the TV, he accepted a couple of pain tablets and three cookies, he complimented Emily and poked at Will. That was like Las Vegas, too, the way the two couples meshed with such ease.

Izzy truly relaxed for the first time since moving into Owen's house.

All four of them were smiling as Will and Emily bid Owen goodbye. Izzy followed them down the flights of stairs, all the way outside to Will's truck.

"Oh, I almost forgot," Emily said, whipping around. "I brought you something."

"A present?" Izzy grinned. "For me?"

Emily's mouth turned down in a grimace. "Well, not exactly a present, but maybe things you'll be just as happy to see."

"Huh?"

Will was already scooping a cardboard box out of the bed of the truck. Emily leaned in to grab another and place it on top. "I'll put them in the living room," Will said, starting off again.

Izzy watched him with resignation. "Are those what I think they are?"

"Hey," Emily said. "You should be happy to get the clothes. I hope they'll be suitable for this climate, but they should be fashionable, since you just shipped them to me to hang on to right before we went to Vegas. The other box is full of books, I think. I've had it for a few years."

"Right," Izzy said. "Thanks."

"What's the matter?"

"Nothing." What could she say? She couldn't complain. There were more than half a dozen friends all over the country who never refused her request to store some stuff for her. And she probably could use the clothes.

"Iz?"

"I'm good. Thanks," she said with false brightness. "You've done me a huge favor!"

Emily was looking at her with suspicious eyes. Izzy made her mouth stretch wider into a big smile. Her relaxing respite was over, but her best friend didn't need to know that. Izzy didn't want anyone to know how much it dismayed her to think of her belongings catching up with her—especially at Owen's.

Chapter Five

Owen was enticed down one flight of stairs by the smell of some kind of simmering sauce that had to include tomato, onion, garlic and basil. Two days had passed since Will and Emily's visit, and he was damn tired of the four walls of the master bedroom suite. He'd started watching medical programs on the Discovery Channel, and the odd conditions highlighted by some of the shows were starting to seriously disturb him.

He found his wife in a corner of the living room, her back turned to the staircase as she bent over a couple of cardboard boxes. Her position tightened her khaki pants across her backside and Owen smiled to himself. Yeah. Way better view than what was available upstairs.

Settling on the last step, he gave himself a few minutes to indulge in a purely masculine occupation—appreciating the physical charms of a beautiful woman. He wasn't going to feel guilty about it, either. For God's sake, he was a guy after all, a bored one at that, and it wasn't a crime that Isabella Cavaletti's sex appeal could spark a pleasant smolder in the center of his libido.

He might be down, but he wasn't dead.

Two days ago her attractions had been stretching his nerves thin, but since that visit from their respective best friends, Izzy had been more businesslike. Instead of her cheerful chatter, she'd turned quiet and polite—downright preoccupied.

He'd decided against prying into her change of disposition. It was no concern of his.

So he could just sit on the step and ogle the outside of her appealing package and leave her inside alone. His gaze followed the line of her spine as she went from bent over to cross-legged on the floor beside the boxes. She reached inside one and pulled out a hardback book. Her shiny black hair swung forward on each side, the split revealing a patch of smooth skin at the nape of her neck.

The spot looked soft and vulnerable and was perfectly sized for a man's mouth. He let his mind wander to the idea, his hand rubbing the stubble on his jaw. If he were smooth shaven, he might place a kiss there, as his hands slid down her sides to her slim hips. She would be warm and pliant as he drew her back against his body, crossing his arms over her flat belly so that rounded butt of hers was tucked against his hips.

As she sensed his erection just layers of denim and cotton behind her, she'd push back, giving her hips a little wiggle while making a sound that was supposed to be a moan, but was much closer to a sob…

A sound that was supposed to be a moan but was much closer to a sob?

Where the hell had that come from? But

then he knew, because he heard it again—Izzy's shoulders trembled and she let out another quiet, choked-off sob.

"Izzy?" he said, without thinking. "Is everything okay?"

She whipped around, and that's when he realized maybe he should have thought first. Maybe he should have thought to take himself back upstairs and leave her to whatever was on her mind. He wasn't supposed to be concerned with the inside of her package even though it was fairly obvious that from the spiky-lashed and tear-drenched chocolate of her eyes, Izzy wasn't too happy.

"How did you get down here?" she asked.

"One stair at a time," he admitted. "On my ass."

"Owen!" she started to scold, then, apparently realizing there were tears on her cheeks, she dashed them away with the backs of both hands. "Owen, you shouldn't be doing that on your own."

"I've been on my own a lot the past couple of days," he heard himself grumble. Oh, hell. Now he sounded like he was complaining about her lack of attention when he'd been wishing for that very thing since he'd let her back into his life.

She made a face. "I'm sorry, I know you must be bored. I've just felt a little less... talkative than usual."

He was such a rat. There she was with tears still drying and she was apologizing to *him*. "What's the matter, honey?"

"Nothing." She shook her head, and

scooted around on her bottom to face him. "Not a thing."

He glanced at the book in her lap, then flicked his gaze toward the boxes behind her. "What do you have there?"

"Oh. Emily brought them over. She's been storing the boxes for me. One contains some clothes and the other a bunch of books from my childhood."

"Yeah? What's the one you have there?" Curiosity about a book wasn't curiosity about *her,* he told himself.

She held it up. "*Eight Cousins,* by Louisa May Alcott. One of my favorite books as a kid, along with the sequel, *Rose in Bloom.*"

He knew Louisa May Alcott, of course, but he had never heard of these two titles. "Does some annoyingly good little girl die?"

She put a hand on her chest and made a mock gasp. "Are you referring to Beth in *Little Women?* For shame, to cast aspersions on one of the most beloved fictional characters of all time. I cried for hours when I read that book the first time."

"Yeah? Well, boys, when they are forced to read that book or watch that movie, we use our imaginations to invent ways to hurry that dreary thing to her ultimate destination." But Izzy had mentioned crying, so he figured he could bring it up. "*Eight Cousins* must have a storyline like that one if you're teary-eyed now."

An embarrassed flush crawled up her neck, and she made another quick swipe at her cheeks. "No, no. It's a cheerful story about an orphan girl who is taken in by her large family and becomes a much beloved member—particularly by the seven boy cousins she's never met before."

"So why'd it make you cry?"

Her gaze slid away from his. "Call me sentimental. I haven't seen this copy in a long time and it reminded me of how much pleasure I got out of reading it as a child."

Remembrance of pleasure would make her sob? It didn't jive, but hey, he'd promised himself he wouldn't pry.

So he lifted his head and sniffed the air. "Something smells really good." He remembered in Vegas that she mentioned coming from a large Italian family, no surprise given her last name and the Mediterranean warmth of her olive skin and big brown eyes. "Is that something from your childhood, too? A woman named Cavaletti surely learned her talent in the kitchen at a young age."

"Both my *nonnas* and a *zia* or two could make a grown man weep with what came out of their stock pots."

Weep? Hmm, more crying. "Yeah? What about your mom? Or is she a rebel like you and skipped out on the cooking lessons?"

"She skipped out on a lot of things," Izzy murmured, but then her gaze narrowed. "Did you just call me a rebel?"

"Ms. Just-Say-No-to-Dewey? What do you think?"

"I think you might be right. Though, truly, moving on from Dewey is—" Breaking off, she laughed. "Don't get me started on the Dewey decimal system. We'll be here all night and I won't even notice your eyes glazing over."

"So what will we talk about then? I *am* bored."

"I don't know." She tucked her hair behind her ears and he found himself fascinated with the tiny gold ring threaded through the rim of her left one.

Rebel, all right. No run-of-the-mill piercing for Isabella Cavaletti. She had a different kind of adornment, one that made him think of that sweet delicate shell of ear and how if he let himself follow it with his tongue, he could suck on her tender lobe without getting a mouthful of jewelry.

It would just be a mouthful of Izzy.

Clearing his throat, he shifted on the step, then shifted his gaze off her pretty face.

"Um…uh…" The boxes. He shook his head, trying to clear it. "Why do you have Emily storing your stuff?"

"Oh." She looked embarrassed again. "Would you believe I don't have my own place?"

He blinked at her. "What?"

"I shamelessly take advantage of my friends, and every one of them ends up with a box or two or three of Izzy-belongings. My work means that I travel all over and I don't have an actual home base, if you know what I mean."

No. He had no idea what she meant. "You don't… you don't have an address?"

"I have a P.O. box, but I take care of my bills online. It seems odd to a lot of people, but it works out fine for me."

"What about…" He couldn't wrap his mind around it. "Television. Car. Coffemaker."

"I rent a car when I need one. Most hotel rooms come complete with TV and coffee service."

Still… "You *are* a rebel. Or should I say a rolling stone?"

Izzy shrugged. "Good phrase. I use it myself. I'm definitely footloose, that's for sure. I travel all over the country and enjoy the different sights I see and the friends I make."

Yeah, but for how long did she enjoy them? She moved from place to place and, unlike a turtle, didn't even bother carrying her house on her back. He remembered Bryce had told him that Izzy had arrived at the condo with only a single small suitcase.

"So you really like living like that?"

"It's good," she said, sounding defensive. "It's a good life."

"I guess." If you didn't like roots or stability or your very own Wii game system. Not to mention a place where your relatives could track you down... Okay, maybe he could see an upside.

But he suspected Izzy couldn't see a thing, because her gaze was back on her copy of *Eight Cousins* and he could detect the distinct glint of tears in her eyes again. He found himself scooting back a step, and cursing his boredom again, because coming down the stairs and seeking her out had been a mistake. What he'd seen and heard—what he'd found inside Izzy—was hitting him right where he didn't want her anywhere near.

His heart.

* * *

In the master bedroom suite, Izzy took plates off the tray that Bryce had carried up the stairs and passed them to the two brothers who were sitting at places set on a card table she'd found stashed in a closet. Bryce pretended to swoon as he breathed in the smell of the lasagna that she'd made from the sauce she'd simmered two days before.

"I love your pretty fairy wife," he told Owen. "She's beautiful, she cooks and she even told me I don't have to worry about doing the dishes later."

"Stop flirting," his brother answered. "And damn right you're going to do the dishes."

Bryce groaned. "Me and my big mouth. Would it aid my cause if I complained about the looooong board meeting Granddad presided over today? I doodled through an entire pad of paper."

Izzy pulled out her chair and sank into her seat as Owen gave Bryce a considering look. "The day you waste time doodling is the day I put on ballet slippers and dance in *Swan Lake*."

Bryce clapped his hands over his ears. "Not another word. Don't burn that image onto my brain!"

Owen glanced at Izzy. "Bryce can take in the details of a meeting, plan another and write up the report on a third all at the same time."

"Not to mention managing my fantasy baseball team," Bryce said, around a bite of lasagna. "Oh, God, this is good, Izzy. Really, I'm *so* marrying you."

She had to smile at him. "But I'm already married."

Bryce's eyes brightened. "About that…"

"Don't go there," his brother warned.

Don't go there. But they had gone there, Izzy thought, for no less than a thousand times, and then had not even gone on to discuss the next step—an annulment—since she'd moved into Owen's condominium. Of course, they'd been pretty much keeping to their corners these days. Though she knew Owen was going stir-crazy, she hadn't felt much like being his entertainment or distraction. That box of books that Emily had delivered seemed to sit on Izzy's shoulders, weighing her down. It was good to have Owen's brother here to give them both another focus.

"Did you hear that, Isabella?"

She started, directing her attention toward Bryce again. "What?"

"I was saying that you two have a reprieve from the Marston machine even when the 'rents get back from their cruise. Right after, Mom's on tap for a benefit she's organizing and she's roped Dad into helping her with the last-minute details."

Izzy thought of the elegant older woman. "Something for the symphony, I suppose?"

"Nah," Bryce answered. "She abhors the symphony."

Owen smiled, and Izzy instantly noticed. He hadn't been doing much of that lately, and it looked good on him. He had strong white teeth and the smile crinkled the corners of his eyes.

"Mom has the pearls and the blue blood, but to give her credit, she's no snob," he said. "She really abhors the symphony just as much as she loves the opera, Springsteen and the Stones." He looked over at Bryce.

"She's a piece of work," they said together, then laughed.

"Dad's favorite phrase," Owen explained.

The brothers shared a smile that forced Izzy to stare down at her plate and swallow a sigh. There was a wealth of family memories and familial closeness in the way Owen and Bryce spoke to each other and spoke about their parents. It made her want to grab a book and escape like she'd done so many times as a child. Inside the pages of a story, she wasn't the outsider, the charity case, the person others felt sorry for.

Even if the book was about an orphan like Rose of *Eight Cousins* and *Rose in Bloom,* the character wasn't left to fend for herself. In books, Izzy had always found her happy ending right along with the protagonist.

"By the way, I thought of another one," Owen said, reaching across the table to touch her arm with his hand.

She looked up. "Another one?" His gaze was trained on her face and she wondered if that was concern she saw in his eyes. It made her skin feel hot and she was suddenly aware of his fingertips on her wrist. Each pad sent an individual streamer of sensation up her arm that then ribboned around her body. Her now-tight lungs struggled to bring in a breath. "Another one what?"

A little smile playing at his mouth, he sang

softly, to the tune of "Rudolph the Red-Nosed Reindeer." "You'll go down and hit a tree."

"Hey," Bryce said, frowning. "Are you making fun of me?"

Owen grinned. "Just how you mangled the words to your favorite Christmas carol. And remember this other immortal line of the same song you misheard—not to mention mis-sang? 'Olive, the other reindeer.'"

"Oh, yeah. For years, I never could figure out why Olive didn't make it into the movie."

Owen shook his head. "Olive the reindeer, lost on the cutting room floor. No wonder I've always been considered the brainy brother in the family."

"Hah!" Bryce said, but he looked stymied for a comeback.

Izzy had to laugh, her low mood rising. Was that what Owen had been after? Was he attuned to her that closely? She rallied, trying to fit in with the lighthearted conversation.

It was what she'd done from childhood, after all—making a small place for herself where none was before. "They're called Mondegreens, you know," she told the two men.

"What?" Bryce asked.

"Misheard lyrics. In 1954, a woman named Sylvia Wright wrote a magazine article confessing that she'd misheard the lyric of a folk song about an unlucky earl, 'and laid him on the green,' as 'and Lady Mondegreen.'"

"Ah," Bryce answered. "So there's a name

for the infamous line Owen once sang at summer camp—'He's got the whole world in his pants.'"

Izzy decided to be loyal and stifled her laugh. "Hey, I know someone who for years thought the refrain for that old TV show theme song was 'The Brady Sponge, the Brady Sponge.'"

"No one could be that dim," Owen scoffed. Then he did a double take, his gaze narrowing on her face. "Wait, the 'someone' was you?"

Heat shot up her face. "I was, like, six or something."

"Yeah, but 'The Brady Sponge'? And you said you sang it that way for years. At least Caro and I clued in Bryce right away about Rudolph not hitting a tree."

"Yeah, but you let me wonder about Olive for half my life," his brother grumbled.

Once again, their exchange tickled Izzy's funny bone. She let herself laugh now, appreciating the echoes of amusement on the faces of the men sharing her table. She was good at this "fitting in and making others feel comfortable" thing—no matter how temporary the circumstances for it were.

"Really, Izzy," Owen said, shaking his head. "I'm trying to wrap my mind around this, because it would seem to be a family-wide shame that should have been corrected immediately. What kind of siblings let you sing 'The Brady Sponge'?"

Oh. "I thought you knew. I'm an only child." And for all *Zia* Sophia or *Nonna* Angela knew, it *was* "The Brady Sponge."

The only programs the elderly ladies watched on TV were *The Price Is Right* and their afternoon soaps.

Owen frowned. "I wasn't aware."

"Probably because he heard an Italian last name and assumed—well, we all know how wrong assumptions can be," Bryce said, his expression pious. "I, on the other hand, make it my pleasure to learn a woman—um, a person—on an individual basis."

"Stop, Bryce," Owen said. "Before I backhand you with my cast."

"I'll tell Mom," his younger brother taunted.

"And I'll—"

"Stop, stop," Izzy cut in, amused by their brotherly byplay. As always, what she'd never had fascinated and bemused her.

"Bryce, your brother's assumptions, if he actually had any, are not that far off the mark. There's a gazillion Cavalettis. Grandparents, great aunts, uncles, aunts and cousins."

"Eight?" Owen asked softly.

Her gaze dropped and she toyed with her fork, unwilling to let him see how his ability to connect the dots of her life made her just a little…nervous. "Close," she said. "They're all quite a bit older, though." And then there were *Zia* Sophia and *Nonna* Angela, who were so old they thought girls still wore girdles and garter belts.

Owen's fingers tangled with hers on the tabletop. "So you were the runt of the litter?" His smile was kind. "Though I can't imagine you being down for long."

That was her secret weapon. Never letting

anyone see that she was down. Pretending, whether it was from within the pages of a book or within the home of some semireluctant relative, had been Izzy's strength against insecurity. "Nobody can resist me for long," she asserted.

Owen's fingers tightened on hers. "I'm a living example," he said mildly.

Bryce shot up from his seat. "Maybe I should get going on those dishes and then let myself out," he said.

"No." Panic fluttered in Izzy's chest. "No, Bryce. I made apple cobbler for dessert. You have to stay for that." *You have to stay and be the buffer between me and Owen.* Though she knew he was desperate for entertainment, it was dangerous to allow it to be *that* kind of entertainment.

"Stay, Bryce," Owen ordered, his voice soft, his gaze fixed on Izzy's face.

Bryce stacked the plates. "Fine. I'll take these downstairs and bring up—"

"You'll take those downstairs, load the dishwasher, do whatever scrub is necessary on the pots and pans and *then* bring up dessert," Owen said.

Without further comment, Bryce took the dirty dishes down the stairs. Owen looked after his brother's retreating figure. "How much I enjoy playing the older brother card."

Izzy smiled. "You didn't have to. I don't mind dishes."

"But I find that at this moment I mind being deprived of your company." He toyed with her fingers, braiding his with hers, unbraiding them, braiding them again. She felt every stroke and tickle, the nerve endings between her fingers seeming to stand on alert to absorb every cell-to-cell contact.

Her breath shortened and she felt her breasts swell and the tips tingle. Did he notice?

"I see what's going on with you," he said.

She twitched. "What?"

"You work too hard, Isabella," he said. "Food, chat, flirtation with my brother." The smile in his blue eyes said he was joking about that last bit. "You're here with me, your husband. You don't have to pretend anything."

But she'd pretended most of her life! Pretended feeling secure, pretended not minding being left behind by her parents, pretended a cheerful, friendly, you-can-be-comfortable-with-me attitude. She was supposed to be all that for Owen while he recuperated from his injuries. The runaway bride owed him that, after all.

"You don't owe me anything," he said.

Did he read minds, too?

His fingers curled around hers, held tight. "Are you okay?"

"I...I don't know," she heard herself whisper. But that wasn't right, because until she met Owen, Isabella Cavaletti always knew that the way to keep others happy was to appear to be happy herself. The girl someone took in—and this wasn't all that different, was it?—couldn't afford to become demanding or temperamental.

She steeled her spine and drew her hand away from Owen's. "I'm completely fine."

He studied her face. "You've got that down pat."

Her heart seemed to sort of cave in on itself. No one had ever detected how often she acted a part. "I don't—"

Owen put two fingers over her mouth.

Okay, it really shouldn't feel like a kiss.

It felt like a kiss.

"You've been alone too long, Iz," Owen said. His hand dropped from her lips and then he was leaning across the corner of the small table so that his mouth was just a breath from hers.

"Not now. Now I'm not alone, Owen." Her skin rose in bumps as if she were experiencing a cold breeze, while her skin actually felt fevered. "I'm…I'm here with you."

He smiled against her mouth. "Exactly."

But before the promise of a kiss could take her away from reality, Bryce saved the day. He strode back into the room. "Who's ready for sweets?"

Chapter Six

As he drifted off to sleep that night, Owen was aware that Bryce had interrupted a crucial moment by bringing in the apple cobbler. During that meal with his brother he'd realized that despite her runaway status, not only was Izzy sexually attractive to him, but he also plain *liked* the woman. Her good humor, her knowledge of odd facts—Mondagreen!—and her moments of emotional vulnerability appealed to him on more than just the libido level.

As Bryce left that evening, she'd kissed him on the cheek. When she'd wished Owen good-night shortly afterward, she hadn't touched him at all.

Which made him admire her brains, too. When the most permanent thing in a woman's life was her P.O. box, then she had no business getting too tangled up in the man with whom she shared a marriage certificate.

They were really going to have to do something about that, he thought, closing his eyes....

He was standing on the roof of a burning structure. Adrenaline pumped through his veins as it did during any firefight. But there was an added kick to the natural drug flooding his system, because this time, he knew. This time, he was keenly aware that at any moment he'd take an elevator fall and drop into the maw of a many-tongued beast roaring in the depths below his fireproof boots.

Jerry was going to fall with him.

He peered across the roof and through the smoke toward his friend. Maybe he could warn him. "Jerry! Jerry!"

His gaze found the other man. Oh, God. His heart shuddered. Jerry was out of uniform! Instead of being protected by full turnout gear as Owen was, the other man was in jeans and a T-shirt. Were those flip-flops on his feet?

Owen started yelling again through his mask. "Jerry! Get the hell off the roof! Jerry! Jerry!"

His buddy looked up, finally heeding Owen's frantic calls. A grin broke over his grimy, ash-darkened face. He gave Owen a jaunty salute, and then—

The roof opened like the gates of hell and Jerry was gone.

"Jerry!" Owen scrambled toward where he'd last seen his friend, but felt the surface beneath his feet give. He was going down, too. His stomach rose toward his throat as he fell. Bad, he thought. This was going to be—

He jerked awake.

Disoriented, breathing hard, he jackknifed to a sitting position. It was darkness surrounding him. Not smoke. Not fire.

His bed. His bedroom. He'd survived.

Only Jerry was dead.

He fell back to his pillows and flopped his forearm over his eyes. God. His mouth was dry and he felt as if he'd just finished a five-mile run with Will and Jerry dogging his every step as they always did during physical training.

But Jerry would never run another step.

Owen groaned, squeezing his eyes tighter shut, though aware that couldn't stop the replay of his dream and of Jerry, that second before he'd fallen through the roof. His grin. His happy-go-lucky wave.

His death.

Owen shoved the covers aside, needing to get out from under their suffocating weight. He swung his legs over the side of the bed. He needed more air, water, something.

Before Bryce had left that night, he'd

moved the furniture to give Owen objects set at strategic distances apart so he could use them for support as he hobbled to the bathroom. He reached for the first, but instead of his fingers finding the edge of the bedside table, his cast swiped the lamp. It hit the floor with a deafening crash.

"Damn!" he cursed, then dropped back to the mattress. There wasn't much hope that Izzy hadn't heard the noise. He had no doubt that she'd come running.

The light in the hallway between the bedrooms snapped on. There was a pattering of footsteps, then his door popped open. "Owen!"

"I'm fine," he said, maneuvering himself beneath the blankets again. "I'm sorry I woke you."

She took a few steps inside the room. "What happened?"

"I'm clumsy," he said, glancing over at her. Then his heart stopped. He didn't know what he would have thought Izzy would wear to bed. A T-shirt big enough for a line-backer? A granny nightgown?

Even his libido couldn't have come up with something like this. Below her tumbled hair, her body was mostly uncovered in a pair of babydoll pajamas—he knew the term from a long-ago former girlfriend who'd worked at a lingerie store—that was a filmy, spaghetti-strapped top worn over a matching pair of boy shorts.

She must have noticed his sudden, tongue-hanging- out interest. Her bare feet shuffled a step back as one arm flew up to cover her chest. "I pack light and I pack, um, little," she said. "I get, uh, hot at night."

"I'm not touching that remark. And don't look so nervous, because I'm not planning on touching you, either," he said, scowling. Just before he'd nodded off, he'd been glad he'd managed to keep his mitts off her, right? Though that was certainly the last of the sleep he'd get tonight, thanks to the disturbing nightmare followed by this chaser of an electrical jolt to his libido.

"Can I get you something?" she asked.

"Water, if you wouldn't mind," he said, trying to sound more human. "There's a glass in the bathroom—and my robe on the back of the door."

In a few minutes she was back, and she handed him the full glass and then leaned down to pick up the lamp and replace it on the table. His flannel robe was belted around her waist and its hem hit her shins. He breathed a sigh of relief, and then another when she straightened. The plaid lapels criss-crossed at her throat, effectively covering her from neck to nearly toes.

He downed half the water in one chug and then set the glass on the bedside table. "Thanks. And again, sorry to have disturbed you."

She stared down at him. "You're not going to be able to get back to sleep, are you?"

"It doesn't matter."

"But it does matter." She sat on the edge of his mattress. "You need a lot of rest because your body's been traumatized, not to mention your psyche—"

"Psyche?" he scoffed. "I'm a man, sweetheart. I don't have a psyche."

She didn't even pretend to find him funny. "Your mind, then. When a friend dies like that—"

Something hot rose from his belly like a red tide. "I told you to stay out of my head, Izzy." Yeah, he was physically weakened, not to mention impotent against the damn dreams and the dark moods that were blanketing him, but he didn't want her pecking at his broken pieces. "Just go away."

He knew he sounded like an abrupt, ungrateful SOB again. Just what he was.

With only the light from the hall filtering into the room, he couldn't read her expression. Her body language said "stubbornly staying," as she didn't move her cute little butt an inch. "How about a bedtime story?"

"For God's sake," he ground out.

"No, really. Let me tell you about Melvil Dewey. Did you know he was instrumental in siting the 1932 Winter Olympics in Lake Placid, New York?"

"Never knew, never cared," Owen answered.

His dismissal didn't dismiss her. For a second he'd thought he'd won his solitude, because she stood up. But then she made her way around the king-size mattress to the other side of the bed. Under his astounded gaze, she propped the pillow against the headboard and stretched out beside him. There was a healthy thirty inches or so between them, but hell, they were sharing the same bed!

"Well, then this should have you snoring in no time," she continued calmly, as she crossed her legs at the ankles. "While Melvil was working in the library at Amherst, he started designing a hierarchical system for the books that would classify all human knowledge. He came up with the decimal-based scheme. There are ten top-tier or 'main' classes that are divided into ten subordinate sections. Each one of those one hundred subordinate topics are broken into ten more divisions. That's a thousand sections that can be referred to by an integer. And each of these numbers can be infinitely divided again using fractional numbers. Now…"

He tuned her out then, though the fact was his attention had begun to wander when she'd said "decimal-based scheme." Not that he had anything against numbers. But with her so close, her slender figure flat against the same mattress that supported him, he could only think of her body. He could only think of that slip of nightwear she wore beneath his utilitarian robe. It was apricot colored, he thought, which reminded him of Bryce's chocolate-and-apricot fairy, which only made him think of all the flavors of Isabella Cavaletti. The ones he knew, and the ones he'd yet to sample.

The disturbing nightmare, his frustration over his physical condition and her irritating stubbornness over not leaving him alone with his sleeplessness, all of those were receding as Izzy took over the forefront of his focus. He could smell a faint note of her perfume, he could sense the warmth of her skin just a few inches away, he could hear her words wash over him, which made his mind jump to her mouth and the way it felt against his. Pillowy soft, with that wet heat inside.

Oh, God. That made him think of Izzy's other hot, wet places. His erection hardened to full arousal.

One wrist was in a cast, and he couldn't put his full weight on his feet, but there was another part of him that was obviously in fine working order. And he couldn't help heeding its sudden, insistent call to action.

Setting his teeth against the erotic ache, he reached over with his good arm and found her hand with his. She jumped a little at his touch, but he soothed her by brushing his thumb across the top of her knuckles.

"Um, Owen?"

He caressed her hand again. "Keep going. I'm listening." *I'm lying, but what the hell?* Because he could tell her temperature was climbing and he could hear the way her breath was coming quicker in response to his hand on hers. This was the instant magic they'd made in Las Vegas. Toying with the cuff of the robe she wore, he pushed it farther up her arm and let his fingertips drift after it, tracking a line from her wrist to the tender inside of her elbow.

Her breath caught. He let his hand drift back, trailing it to her fingers and then back up again.

Her legs made a restless movement, the edges of the robe opening to reveal her bare legs to a point just above her knees. His blood surged in his veins, as if she'd suddenly gone naked.

His gaze traced the olive skin as if he were licking a line down her shin. Her legs moved again, and the robe revealed another few inches of Izzy's thighs. Without thinking, he slid his hand around one of them, cupping the taut muscle on top and letting his fingers press against the sleek inner surface.

He heard her swallow, then she valiantly continued with her sleep-inducing—hah!— lecture. "I think you'll like this part the most," she said. "He was an advocate for a simpler spelling system for the English language. At one point he considered writing his own name as *M-E-L-V-I-L D-U-I.*"

He moved his hand, stroking her leg now,

and saw the way her thighs parted ever more. Under the pads of his fingers, he felt her telltale goose bumps.

"Um, Owen?" she said again, her voice fainter this time. "Do you… Are you… What are you thinking?"

Of only one thing, for good or for bad. Only one damn thing. "I'm thinking ol' Melvil would completely approve," he said, "when I tell you that I would like to *H-A-V S-E-X*."

Izzy's heart was beating harder than it had in those few seconds after she'd heard the crash of Owen's lamp and made it to his bedroom to discover he was all right. Her skin was tingling from the slow washes of goose bumps rolling from the point where he touched her thigh. *H-A-V S-E-X,* her brain repeated.

Desire had been pooling low in her belly from the instant he touched her hand, and at that thought—having sex with Owen—the heaviness there throbbed.

"We shouldn't... We don't... But..."

"Yeah," he whispered, his hand still tracing mysterious patterns on her skin. "All that."

"Then why?"

"Because it's a long, dark night. Because I remember what it felt like to dance with you in Vegas, and I think we'll do this dance well, too. Because I could do with a little human contact." He rolled on his side, and he lifted his casted wrist so those fingers could brush the hair off her forehead. "Take your pick, Isabella."

His palm flattened on her thigh, and he leaned close to press his mouth briefly to hers. "Take your pick or say no. Whichever you want."

But it was never the way she wanted! She'd spent the last few years trying to make things her way after a childhood of being passed off and shuffled over, in a manner that made her feel she had to be quiet or accommodating or easy to get along with, whatever the new living situation required of her. Only since she'd started her career in library consultation had she really been able to order her world the way that pleased *her*.

And she'd never wanted to want a man like she wanted Owen Marston.

But she did want him, and here he was, just inches away, his gentle touch sparking blazes along her nerve endings, like those signal fires that ancient peoples used to spread news.

Of good tidings?

Of danger ahead?

"Just a little human contact," he whispered again, and her heart squeezed, ridding itself of the last of her objections.

It was the thing she needed, too—and often. Human contact, human comfort—the loving touch of a parent, even the playful shove of a sibling—would have been welcome during those lonely childhood years. Books were magic, and they had taken her away and given her hundreds of new worlds and new characters to be—but they couldn't provide the warmth of a body. They were not a substitute for the strength and heat of a man to whom she wanted to offer her matching softness and need.

So here was a temptation she wasn't willing to pass up. An opportunity to share the long night with someone who made her insides tremble with just the briefest of kisses. But *brief* was the operative word. They'd been briefly in the same orbit, they were going to be briefly married and this interlude of contact and comfort would be brief, too.

Brief, lightweight, not meaningless, but not full of heavy implications, either. It would be a pleasurable way for two people to fill a long, dark night.

He traced her upper lip with two fingers and she tilted her chin to catch the pads between her teeth. She felt him tense, and when she licked across his skin, he groaned an answer to her caressing tongue. His other hand left the inside of her thigh and traveled to her far hip so that he could roll her toward him. In a smooth jerk, their bodies were flush.

She sucked on his fingers and he groaned again, pulling them free of her mouth so he could use the damp tips to paint her lips. "This was the first thing I noticed when I met you. Soft and full and the color of summer plums."

"I was wearing a bikini, and you were looking at my *face?*" she teased. Teasing, smiling, flirtatious. That was just the way she wanted this interlude to go.

"The second time you were wearing a bikini," he reminded her, "and I promise I was suitably impressed." The back of his hand skimmed her throat and then followed the center of her body to subtly loosen the belt around her waist. "But the first occasion we met was over drinks, and I think we were both a little put out that our two friends had dragged us to meet a total stranger."

"Oh, not me. Emily always connects me with the cutest hunks. I can't tell you how many pickups she's found for me at these librarian conventions."

He punished her sass by leaning in and biting her lower lip. She squealed a fake protest as a hot arrow shot from her mouth to her womb. "Hey, don't damage the kisser."

His hands paused in the middle of stripping the robe off her shoulders. "'Don't damage the kisser'? Is that librarian-speak?"

"It's…it's…" She had no idea what it

was, because the pathway from the thinking part of her brain to its speech center was suddenly experiencing gridlock. Owen had slid the flannel free of her skin and now the only thing covering her was the filmy fabric of her shortie nightgown and matching panties—and the heat of Owen's gaze.

He cupped one breast and rolled his thumb across the already hard tip. The flesh tightened and she felt herself swelling, become even more sensitive with each light pass of his thumb. "Owen…" she breathed.

"The second thing I noticed about you," he said, "was that you have a strong reaction to cold."

"What?" She wanted to laugh, or maybe she wanted to hit him. "That was the second thing you noticed? Do men really pay attention to…to…stuff like that?"

One corner of his mouth kicked up. "My brothers-in-slavedom-to-our-sex-drives might not appreciate me admitting this, but, yes, we really pay attention to 'stuff' like that. Right next to *dog* in your library's fat fancy dictionary, you're likely to find a photo of a guy who looks just like me."

He'd not stopped stroking her nipple during the confession, so she had a difficult time being as appalled or offended as she supposed she should be. Instead, she found herself leaning toward him, silently begging for more than that subtle touch.

"What can you tell me about women?" he whispered, his mouth tracing her eyebrow, the rise of her cheekbone, the line of her jaw.

"Is there some confession you'd like to share?"

She tried to come up with something funny or teasing or fun, but all she could think about was the tingling tip of her breast and the maddening way he was really not even touching it. Yes, not really touching it at all, she realized, as her focus centered on the movements of his maddening thumb. His flesh wasn't making contact with hers. His palm barely cradled her breast, and his thumb was merely moving the gauzy fabric of her nightwear across her hard nipple.

"Isabella? A confession?"

Enough of fun, funny, teasing. "If you don't really touch me, Owen, I'm going to scream."

Instead of obeying, he let out a low, sexy laugh, then rolled again, landing flat on his back, with her on top of him. "So at least I know a little more about Isabella. She's demanding, impatient, single-minded…"

He was the one teasing now. But she was miffed at him anyway for being so in control when she was so obviously losing her grasp on her dignity. She rose up, a knee on either side of his hips, determined to put a little distance between them.

Owen stole that determination away as he instantly scooted down on the mattress and took her nipple in his mouth. Surprise short-circuited her brain. Her body arched, her shoulders jerking back and her bottom shooting up. He groaned against her flesh, sucking harder as his casted arm lay across the small of her back and his other palm cupped the raised curve of her behind.

He took his mouth from her and she moaned. "We're not done, sweetheart," he said. "I promise. But you're going to have to help me out again, Isabella. As much as I'd like to strip you myself, my cast will just get in the way."

She hesitated, a little shy, a little nervous. He palmed her bottom again. "Isabella, get naked and then I'll take you in my mouth again."

Desire burned through her veins. Her hands shook as she undressed under his watchful gaze. Her stomach fluttered, because naked suddenly didn't seem lightweight or fun or funny. It seemed personal and intimate and maybe more than she could handle if the other human on the end of "contact" was Owen Marston, who had thrilled her from the first moment their eyes had met across the crowded casino.

His hand slid along her ribcage, encouraging her back into position. "Oh, sweetheart. Everything about you is so pretty," he said. She was trembling, but shyness and nerves evaporated the moment he took her breast into his mouth.

Her body bowed again, heat flashed across her skin and Owen groaned as his other hand lifted to toy with her other nipple. Her belly sank lower, brushing against the hard erection she could feel beneath his cotton boxers. She put one hand to the waistband and wiggled her fingers under to find the silky tip.

His hips shifted upward at her touch and

his mouth tightened on her nipple. They both groaned.

His mouth moved between her breasts as she continued to caress him. "Sweetheart," he said suddenly, his voice low and tight. "No more. No more or this will all be over."

But she liked the fact that he was begging her this time, and she rolled off him against his protests, just so she could strip him as naked as she. Then she crawled up the mattress, finding her inner tease again, licking his hair-dusted shin, taking a nip at his knee cap, pressing kisses against his muscled thighs.

His hand found her hair as she pressed baby kisses all around his groin. His fingers bit into her scalp when she wrote a message with her tongue on his hard length. When she reached the tip, he yanked upward on her hair, bringing their bodies flush, their mouths within kissing distance.

Owen Marston had not lost his talent for kissing. He laid them on her, one after one, feeding the sweet drug of intimacy to her, until she was hot and wiggly and so wet and swollen between her legs that when he touched her there with one long finger it slid inside so easily he immediately added another.

They were groaning against each other's mouths, needing no words to share confessions, telling secrets with their bodies and it was all so good, so right, so simple. It was like a "Dui" version of how sex should be, and when he whispered instructions to her, telling her where to find a condom and then telling her to lift up and slide down on him, she didn't feel embarrassed or exposed, or any of the dozens of emotions that moments like this between a man and a woman could sometimes bring.

She only felt pleasure.

Chapter Seven

Owen sat on the edge of the made-up bed to pull on his clothes after his shower. He'd woken alone, but there was the smell of coffee rising up the stairs and a note left on the pillow where Izzy had lain.

It was composed of a single word—a Dui-esque *THNX.*

It made him smile to look at it, and to

think of what had passed between them, when together they'd transformed the cold darkness of his nightmare into the velvet cocoon of shared sexual pleasure. First thing this morning, he needed to convey a "THNX" of his own. She'd been what he'd needed the night before, and this morning he could revel in a sense of well-being he hadn't experienced since before the night of the fire.

He felt like himself again, the laid-back, calm-in-a-crisis, impervious-to-pressure Owen Marston who'd headed out with his head on straight the night of that last call. He wanted to keep a firm grasp on that—and on that man.

From the bedside table, his cell phone rang. He didn't bother checking the screen;

he just put the phone to his ear and then swallowed his groan when he heard the raspy voice coming through the speaker. "Have you cooled down yet?" his grandfather demanded.

Owen recalled that the last time he'd spoken with the old man, he'd hung up on him. It was a minor miracle that Philip Marston had let this long pass without another call. Owen probably owed Bryce a beer or two or twelve for running interference for him.

"I'm good, Granddad," Owen said, swiping Izzy's note from the bedside table and stuffing it into his pocket. She'd apparently made the bed while he was showering, and he was glad she hadn't tossed the scrap of paper. It was tangible proof that he was a man on the mend. "How are you?"

"Annoyed, impatient, concerned."

Owen grinned. "And so self-aware, too. What's got your dander up?"

"Well, you, of course! I promised your mother I wouldn't pester you...."

So it was his mother Owen had to thank for his grandfather's uncharacteristic—though obviously now over—period of radio silence. Unfortunately, she didn't go for the easy beer payoff, which made him more than a little uneasy.

"...but hell," his grandfather continued. "You're my eldest grandson, and it's not like I don't read the newspapers!"

The non sequitur clearly stated the old man was agitated. Usually he was extremely, and sometimes obnoxiously, direct. "Granddad," Owen said, "I'm having a little trouble following you."

"Did you hit your head when you fell?"

"No." He frowned. "I just don't see how me being your eldest grandson and you reading the business pages have anything in common."

"They have everything in common. And it's not the *Wall Street Journal* that I'm talking about. It's the *Paxton Record.*"

Tiny carpenters had invaded Owen's brain and were tapping on his skull with their tiny hammers. He pinched the bridge of his nose between his thumb and forefinger, trying to force the pain away and remember that last night he'd had the best sex of his life. Izzy on top, her warm flank in the palm of his hand, her incredible molten center sliding down on him. The carpenters faded away and he took in a slow breath.

"Did you hear me, son? The *Paxton Record.*"

"You're irritated by the score of the high school football team? I don't think they've been the same since Bryce graduated—"

"This isn't about your brother, who did the right thing and joined the family business. This is about you!"

It's what Owen had been afraid of, ever since the last phone call he'd had from his grandfather, the one during which he brought up the old argument about Owen's career choice. The carpenters set to work again. "Granddad—"

"Did you or did you not go to college intending to join the business?"

"I did. You know I did." Maybe if he let the old man get it out of his system, they could drop this familiar quarrel for good—or at least for now. "And I interned every summer and listened to you talk about the company at every family dinner. But it just wasn't for me."

"How do you know?"

"I know because when I worked there it drained my enthusiasm and my energy. And I know because after the first hour at the fire academy I had found it again." Not only energy and enthusiasm, but purpose and pride. There was nothing wrong with what his father and Bryce and Caro had chosen to do—involve themselves in and expand the business Philip Marston had started. It just wasn't Owen's choice.

"You were good at it," the old man grumbled.

"And Bryce was a damn good quarterback, but you're not all over his case for not trying out for the NFL."

"I told you, this is not about your brother. And damn it, I would have been all over his case if he had set his sights on the NFL. Do you know how many of those players limp off the field with debilitating injuries that affect them for the rest of their lives?"

Owen slid his fingers in his pocket to touch Izzy's note. *Remember last night. Remember that smile on your face this morning.* "Granddad, what does this all have to do with me?"

"I'm coming by to see you today."

"No."

"Nonsense. Would you prevent an old man from assuring himself his favorite grandson is recovering?"

"Bryce is your favorite grandson."

"Today it's you."

Owen rolled his eyes. "I need my rest."

"You're getting plenty of rest. And your mother told me you have a nice health worker living there with you, making sure you don't overtax yourself."

Well, he might have overtaxed himself a little last night… "Wait. What? Health worker?"

"Some young woman. Misty? Betsy?"

"Izzy," Owen corrected, wondering what he was going to owe his mother now. He should have known she'd kept quiet about his marriage or else his grandfather would have been on his doorstep immediately, eager to meet the mother of his great-grand-sons. "Her name is Isabella."

"Well, I assume she's taking good care of you."

He touched the note again, sniffed the coffee in the air and swore that he smelled French toast and maple syrup. "The best."

"So I'll see you in a few minutes."

"What? You're more than an hour away."

"I'm talking to you from the limo. I'm in Paxton right now."

Between the little carpenters and the old man, Owen's good mood was taking a serious beating. "Tell me you're joking."

"Not at all. I want us to have a serious, face-to-face discussion."

Oh, God. "About…?"

"Now that you know the potential consequences of this career of yours, I'm going to persuade you to see reason and quit."

Here they went again. "No."

"A man died, Owen."

"Don't you think I know that?" he burst out. His own loud voice obliterated the last of his well-being. "Don't you realize I can't stop thinking of that?"

Fine. That was the damn truth of it. That Jerry was gone had been hovering over him like a black cloud since he'd come to in the hospital.

That Jerry was gone *and* that Owen hadn't been able to prevent Jerry's death. All his training, all their equipment and experience, none of it had been able to stop the outcome. It was just like that damn nightmare, when even aware of what was about to happen, Owen hadn't been able to stop Jerry from going down.

"And son, I read in the paper…" Philip Marston cleared his throat. "I read in the Paxton newspaper that your colleague, he was younger than you."

"A couple of years."

"And that he was married."

"I went to their wedding," he heard himself say. "The bride's name is Ellie." He thought of her apple cheeks and her sparkling blue eyes. Even in a wedding dress and veil, she'd looked hardly older than a teenager. She and Jerry had been high school sweethearts and he'd worn that same jaunty grin at the altar that Owen had seen on his face in the nightmare.

His grandfather's voice lowered to a gruffer note. "The young widow is eight months pregnant."

The carpenters synchronized their hammers, assaulting Owen's skull with a single joint blow. He squeezed his eyes against the pain. "Yes." Eight months pregnant. Oh, damn it all, yes.

It was that fact he'd been avoiding facing since he'd learned of Jerry's death. It's why he hadn't moved hell and high water to make it to the funeral. It was why he'd not called Ellie, or sent a separate floral arrangement besides the one the station had added his name to and the other that his mother had sent from the entire Marston clan.

He hadn't wanted to think about it.

Jerry had been so psyched to be a dad. He swore he was going to be the kind who read to his toddler every night. He'd coach if the child was into sports, he'd applaud if the kid was into dance recitals, he'd listen to squeaky violin lessons and make a hundred kites catch wind.

Jerry said he'd had that kind of father himself and wanted to give his son or daughter every wonderful childhood moment that he'd experienced. Jerry's dad had passed away five years before. Jerry two weeks ago.

Leaving no one to do all those things for Jerry and Ellie's child because Jerry had died.

And Owen survived.

Why?

He hadn't wanted to ask himself that question because he knew there was no good answer.

Why?

Why?

He forced the question from his mind. "Look, Granddad—"

"I'm walking up your front steps, Owen," the old man said. "You better tell your young woman to let me in."

And remind her not to give away that she was Owen's wife, he thought, hobbling toward the bedroom door. Great. His positive mood was gone for good. He touched the note in his pocket. And now he'd found the perfect way to extinguish hers, too.

Izzy hauled in a deep breath before opening Owen's front door. She knew who was on the other side. Philip Marston. His grandson, the man she'd slept with the night before, had just called her up the stairs in an urgent voice and explained that his grandfather was moments away and that she'd been identified as the "health worker" by his mother. For reasons of their privacy, Owen supposed, or their sanity, he'd added.

He'd looked tense and tired, the exact opposite of how she'd felt upon waking up. She hoped it was the unexpected arrival of his grandfather that was affecting his mood, but…well, she just wasn't going to worry about it. Her state of mind was buoyant, and she planned on keeping it that way.

Why not? She'd been wondering for weeks about what she'd missed out on with Owen, and now she knew. Yes, as he'd suspected, they danced on the mattress as well as they did in the clubs in Las Vegas. Satisfying one's curiosity could be a positive experience.

On her next breath, she pulled open the door. The impression of a tall, gray-haired man flashed through her brain before she found herself flat on her back on the floor, a yellow monster hanging over her.

"Nugget," the man scolded. "Is that any way for a Marston to act?"

The big dog swiped her chin with a wet tongue, then pranced backward to stare at her with big brown eyes. Izzy cautiously sat up.

"Granddad? You brought the dog?"

Izzy glanced back to see Owen on the upper landing. Then she returned her gaze to the canine standing at attention, close enough that she could feel his breath wash over her face.

"It's okay, Izzy," Owen said.

Mr. Marston frowned down at her. "Not afraid of dogs, are you?"

"Um…I don't know any dogs. Not, um, this close and personal, anyway." The elderly ladies she'd most often stayed with had been cat people. She slowly climbed to her feet, and, one eye on the dog, held her hand out to the older man. "I'm Isabella Cavaletti, Mr. Marston."

His shake was brief and businesslike. "Good to meet you. And this champion yellow Labrador is none other than Marston's Golden Nugget."

"Or, as we find more appropriate, the Nug," Owen added.

"Okay," Izzy said. The dog looked more like a "Nug" than a champion. He was still watching her with his doggy eyes and his tongue hanging out. "Would everybody, um, like some breakfast?"

"You're not here to wait on us," Owen started.

His grandfather spoke over him. "Just coffee for me, please. Black. Owen, your mother said you're headquartered upstairs during your recovery. Can I help you back to bed?"

"I don't need to lie down," his grandson grumbled. "But come on up, Granddad."

To her dismay, the dog hung around in the kitchen while she put together a tray. Did he somehow think she was suspect? Could he tell she was a counterfeit "health worker"?

Then she happened to knock a piece of bacon off a plate, sending it toward the floor. Nugget, aka "the Nug," caught it in midair.

She stared at him. "You're not suspicious, you're a mooch."

He didn't appear to take offense. In fact, he kept even closer to her as she put Owen's plate on the tray, the coffees, and then carried the food and beverages up the stairs. She found the two men around the small meal table she'd set up. Trying to remain unobtrusive, she put Owen's breakfast in front of him and then placed the mug of black coffee at Mr. Marston's elbow.

She and the Nug were ready to slink off when Owen caught her wrist. "Stay," he said, his tone soft.

His grandfather glanced up at her. "By all means. Maybe an objective viewpoint is exactly what we need."

Izzy avoided both men's gaze. Objective?

Could she possibly be nonpartisan when she'd spent the night before in Owen's arms? "I, um…" But her protest, such as it was, died, as she lowered herself to the free chair. Even without looking directly into his eyes, she was aware that Owen's tense, tired expression had turned grim. She couldn't ignore that, could she?

He was her husband, after all.

"I'm just explaining to my grandson, here, that it's time to reconsider his choice of career."

Izzy glanced at Owen. "Well—"

"It was fine for a time, but…"

She glanced at Owen again. His face was expressionless. She remembered the conversation he'd had with his mother, when he'd defended his job as a firefighter, but now he didn't look interested in sticking up for himself. "I think he likes his work."

"Because he hasn't truly considered the consequences," Philip Marston said with a wave of his hand. "Young men believe themselves immortal. It's biology. The brain isn't sufficiently formed to foresee the risks of a particular action."

"Well, that's true of many adolescents," Izzy agreed. "But you can't lump into that group every single person who pursues a job that involves some personal risk."

Owen's grandfather's eyes narrowed. "Tell me again how you came to be a home health worker?"

She ignored the question. "We need our first responders. Surely you would admit that."

The elder Mr. Marston frowned. "All first responders aren't my grandson."

Izzy looked over at Owen. It was obvious he wasn't listening to their exchange. His gaze was unfocused and trained on some inner movie screen, and uneasiness trickled down her back. It made her voice sharp. "You don't give your grandson much respect," she said, more direct than her usual Izzy's-here-to-please style. "His work is important."

"Hah." The older man sent her another piercing look. "Well. You're awfully loyal for a temporary, hourly employee."

That caught Owen's attention, and he looked over. "Leave Izzy alone, Granddad."

"What?"

"Leave Izzy alone," Owen ground out.

"I'm not bothering her," his grandfather replied in a mild voice. "Now, Nugget on the other hand…"

She glanced down and had to laugh. She'd been so caught up in the conversation that she hadn't realized the beast was resting his head on her lap. When it came to canines, bacon must hold a special power.

"I don't know anything about dogs." Her hand caressed the buttery fur on the top of his head.

"I thought I explained all about them last night," Owen murmured.

It startled another laugh out of her, but then it died, as "last night" came back to her: Owen's grin, his touch, the intimacy of the darkness and his caresses.

In the silence surrounding them, his

grandfather humphed. "Nothing anyone has said negates my concerns, Owen. Your coworker was killed."

His grandson stilled. "You keep saying that."

"Because it's true."

And Izzy could see the knowledge of it wash over Owen. His posture didn't change— it remained straight and strong—but she could see anguish ripple across his face, deadening the color of his eyes and setting his mouth into a grim line. His gaze unfocused again and she knew he was once again tuning them out.

She leaned forward. "Owen…"

Her voice jerked him out of his reverie. He blinked, his gaze focusing on her. "Jerry's wife, Ellie, is expecting a baby in a few weeks. Maybe any day now, I'm not sure."

"Oh, Owen."

"She's a widow. That baby won't have a father."

"Exactly my point," Philip Marston boomed. "You'll get married soon. You'll have a child. Will you still take the same risks with your life? I say leave now, and get back into the family business where you belong."

You'll get married soon. You'll have a child.

Of course he would. She and Owen would undo their whim of a wedding and he'd find himself a real wife.

That couldn't be her, because she couldn't see herself settling down. She didn't know how to do it. How did anyone trust someone else with their heart?

"Maybe you're right, Granddad," Owen said. "I'll be thinking about that."

Izzy barely heard him. She pushed out of her chair, murmuring something about cleaning up the breakfast dishes. With the Nug dogging her footsteps—so that's where the phrase came from, she thought—she returned to the kitchen. There, she stood, unmoving, as Philip Marston's words repeated in her head.

You'll get married soon. You'll have a child.

Yes, she wasn't part of that picture, was she? She caught sight of her reflection in the silver surface of the refrigerator and her hands went to her belly. Really, she couldn't see herself that way. Pregnant and barefoot? No.

Pregnant and wearing those cute slides she'd spied at Nordstrom the other day? Well…

No!

And…yes.

The dog pressed up against her thigh and she rubbed the top of his head. "I'm crazy, right?" she whispered.

Because there was a picture forming in her mind. Izzy, the perpetual outsider, having her very own family. Being someone's wife.

Owen's wife.

The Nug whined, the sound popping that aberrant mental bubble. With a sigh, she glanced down at the dog. "Yeah, I know. You're hoping for more bacon to fly through the air, and when pigs do that very same thing is when I'll allow myself to rely on someone for that forever-after thing."

On another sigh, she moved to the sink

and started dealing with the dishes, not allowing herself to get caught up in the domestic intimacy of it all. "It may be like playing house," she told the Nug, who continued his crumb surveillance, "but it's not my house, and this is definitely not the way I would play it anyway."

Nobody was supposed to have to cook *and* clean up, after all. "Which just goes to show I'm merely the hired help. The health worker, right, Nug?" Even Owen's mother had figured out Izzy wasn't wife material.

The doorbell rang and she was glad for an excuse to hurry away from her own thoughts. She swung open the door, only to see a mail service truck lumber off. On the doorstep were four large cardboard boxes.

Frowning, she checked the address.

It was Owen's, all right.

But the name on the *To:* line was all wrong.

Isabella Cavaletti Marston.

Chapter Eight

Owen groaned from the easy chair by his bedroom window as he watched his brother stride over the threshold, his arms full of bound reports. "Tell me those aren't what I think they are."

"You told Granddad you were thinking about joining the company," Bryce said, dropping the stack at Owen's feet. "What, you thought he'd forget about that?"

"I didn't think he would have you bring me homework, like you used to do when we were kids and I missed a day of school."

Bryce settled in the matching chair. "You never missed a day of school, remember? Perfect attendance, six years running. God, I hated you for that."

"Wasn't my fault you didn't remember that girls have cooties. That's where all those coughs and colds come from, you know."

"Well, the one who I think is sick now is you. Sick in the head."

Owen narrowed his eyes at his brother. "What do you mean by that?"

With a nod, Bryce indicated the window.

"Why are you up here moping and not down there with her?"

"Down there" was the courtyard they could see below. Izzy had discovered the neighbor's cat sunning itself on the bricks and she was crouched beside the fluffy creature, alternately petting it and letting it bat at a long piece of yarn she held.

"Yeah? What excuse could I give?"

"That you, too, want to pet a—" He broke off at Owen's sharp glance. "You have a dirty mind! I was going to say 'pet a cat.' Yeesh."

"I'll just bet."

Bryce grinned. "Speaking of gambles…I never really got a chance to hear the full story about your whirlwind Vegas, uh, vacation. You went for the adventure and came home with—"

"Nothing," Owen ground out. "You know that."

"But then five weeks later this pretty woman trips into your life and claims she's your wife. Don't you think I've been patient long enough? Don't I get all the details now?"

"Since when are you like a teenage girl at a slumber party?"

"Since you turned so close-mouthed and crotchety."

Bryce said it with his usual smile on his face, but Owen still felt the sting. *Crotchety* sounded old and cranky, and damn if that wasn't the way he felt. "I hate being cooped up."

"But you're cooped up with a babe. C'mon, surely I don't have to spell out ways to lift your mood."

The thought didn't lift Owen's mood. He'd woken up two days ago, feeling about as good as a man could, and then his grandfather had called and he'd remembered what the sex had pushed aside.

Jerry Palmer, imminent father-to-be, was dead.

And Owen still couldn't figure out why he was alive.

"If you're not in any hurry to seduce the lovely Isabella, I think you're going to have to tell me how she ended up as your wife."

Owen stared through the glass at her profile, the smooth curve of her cheek, that plum-colored purse of her mouth. Her fingers swept through the cat's fur and he remembered them buried in his hair as they sank into yet another kiss. "The usual way," he answered. "Elvis asked. We said 'I do.'"

"No. Way." Bryce hooted. "I love it. Golden Boy Marston, Granddad's favorite, the one Mom loves best, the guy Dad envies because he doesn't have to deal with the old man on a daily basis, was married by an *Elvis impersonator?*"

"Who says he was an impersonator? And so you know, Priscilla can play a mean Wurlitzer organ."

Bryce started laughing, hard enough that Owen couldn't stop his own smile. "You're not kidding."

"Would I kid you about the complimentary, postceremony, grilled peanut-butter-and-banana sandwiches?"

"It's so bad, it's good." Bryce leaned close. "Tell me there are pictures."

"There are pictures." He put up his hand to stop his brother's next question. "But no, you can't see them. Izzy took them with her, and knowing her habits, I'd guess they've been shipped to some friend of hers in Timbuktu." Yet, he discovered he was still smiling. As rash as their decision to marry had been that night, he'd enjoyed the hell out of himself the entire time.

From the moment he'd met her, he'd enjoyed the hell out of himself. But who could believe something like that could last?

He had.

"So what happened?"

"Hm?" Owen looked over at his brother.

"What happened? A second ago you were

wearing one of those Perfect Attendance Award smiles and then next thing you look like someone told you the principal was taking away your traffic patrol captain's badge."

He stared at his brother. "You really did hate me during our school years, didn't you?"

"Nah. You've just always been a hell of a brother to follow after. And if you were going to buck the family and go for a job outside the company, why couldn't you have chosen to be a shoe salesman or something? Not that all work isn't honorable, but hell, bro— A firefighter. I'll be in your shadow for the rest of my life."

"You're so full of BS." As if Bryce was in anyone's shadow. "And I don't know how long I'm going to be with the department anyway."

Bryce wagged one foot. "Pull the other one. I don't care what you told Granddad, but you're not leaving the Paxton F.D. *And,* you're not putting me off my slumber party sensibilities. I'm still waiting for the details. What happened between you and your bride that she went running?"

"She went running." Owen spread his hands. "I caught her in the hotel lobby as she was hotfooting it out of the place. She looked scared. I acted certain. She got mad. I got madder. Next thing I know—"

"She doesn't look scared when she looks at you now."

"Yeah, instead she looks sympathetic. I'm her pity project."

Bryce shrugged. "Maybe you need to show her that you still have some moves."

He'd shown her his moves. Moves weren't the problem. Things between them had been good in bed. Better than good. He knew that. But what came after?

He hadn't gone looking for a repeat. And not just because they hadn't resolved or even discussed their marriage. That was just one of the pile of issues that was taking up the front and center of his head.

"Well." Bryce slapped his palms on his thighs. "Gotta go. I delivered your spelling and math as ordered. Except, oh, yeah, there's this little question I believe you should be addressing. In regards to entering the family business: What the hell are you thinking? Write up five cogent paragraphs and get back to me."

He passed Izzy in the doorway, pausing

only long enough to grab her by the shoulders and buss her on the cheek. "Yum. You smell good. When you want the better brother, let me know. In the meantime, I think you should take the big guy over there to the fire station. Someone needs a little face time with his team."

Izzy blinked as Bryce strode away, then came farther into the room. Her eyebrows rose as she took in the mountain of materials that the other man had left behind. "Most people recuperate with lighter reading. I have several recommendations for you. Do you like mysteries? Thrillers? Or, if you're serious about heavier fare, I know a great biography of one of our founding fathers."

"These are some of the company's financial reports," Owen said. "Granddad sent them over."

"You're not really thinking—" She broke off. "But it's none of my business."

"Yeah."

And it was none of his business to absorb how beautiful she was, even in a pair of sweatpants and a T-shirt. Even those brief few minutes in the sunshine had spread a layer of rosy warmth across her cheekbones…or maybe she was thinking, like he was, of how they'd been together that night. Of how the kisses had gone on forever and how seamlessly they'd joined and how he'd felt her orgasm pulsing around him as she came.

Sex had been as easy and as right as that first moment in Las Vegas. As well matched as their dancing. As hot as every glance they'd shared before they'd said "I do" while the rhinestones on Elvis's suit glittered in the disco ball light of the chapel.

She looked out the window. "Is Bryce right? Do you want to go to the fire station?"

The heat kindling inside him went cold. "I don't know if I should go back there." He didn't know if he *could* go back there.

"Owen…"

"What?"

Her gaze stayed trained on the window. "We didn't talk about the other night."

"That's right." He touched the outside of his pocket. He'd made a habit of carrying around her THNX, sap that he was. "I appreciate what you shared with me. That night…it was a tough time."

"I know."

"And you…?"

She shot him a quick glance. "You know darn well I have no complaints."

"Good."

"Good." Her gaze cut his way again. "But…"

"But?"

"Does this need to be said?"

That it could never happen again? That it had been a huge mistake? That he was an idiot for not being able to keep her taste, her scent, the feel of her silky skin out of his head?

He steeled himself. "Does what need to be said?"

"That it's okay to delight in being alive."

"I…I don't know what you mean."

"It's all right to have enjoyed what we did, Owen. It's all right to have enjoyed our…pleasure. You have nothing to feel guilty about."

Owen stared out the window. Would she still say that if she knew? Would she say it was all right if she knew that every cell of him wanted to "delight in being alive" again? Right now. Tonight. Tomorrow.

But that *was* wrong, wasn't it? She was temporarily here. He was temporarily needing her near. And he was afraid that all that "delighting" that he wanted was just an excuse to get away from what really needed to be done: Facing all the questions about his future.

The next day, Owen felt so suffocated by the four walls around him that he gave in and agreed to go to dinner at Will and Emily's house with Izzy. Though he didn't want to talk shop with Will, he was fairly certain he could avoid what was happening down at the station by using the two women as a buffer.

His plan was to settle himself on the couple's couch and keep quiet.

His worries were needless, he realized, when he limped into the house, using the cane that he'd been given by the orthopedist. No one was going to be expecting him to maintain his end of a conversation because there were too many of them going on. He and Izzy were not the only dinner guests. Will's siblings were in attendance, too, along with a variety of spouses, girlfriends and roommates, which made it easy for Owen to hide behind the noise and chaos.

As she'd been doing lately, Izzy wandered

off, leaving him alone. When they were at his place, she didn't hang around him, either. He supposed she read a lot of the time. He knew she talked on the phone often. It rang a heck of a lot—so much that the distinctive ring tone was starting to rub his nerves raw. Probably some of her calls were business related, and he'd brought up the fact that he was causing her trouble on that end—giving her the chance to say she needed to leave him—but she'd waved the concern away.

Too bad he couldn't bring up her other phone calls and have her wave away the concern he had about those, too. But that would mean admitting he'd been listening. That would mean admitting he was a little, um, well, irritated shouldn't be the word, but it was, by the many times she'd been thrilled to hear from "Greg" and "David" and "Brad." Of course, there'd been calls from "Jane" and "Sally" and "Taylor," too, but— but wait, "Taylor" was a name that could go either way, meaning yet another possible hash mark under the column entitled "Male Callers," right?

The sofa cushion beside his bounced as a younger man dropped into the other corner. As tall and dark as his brother, but as skinny as only a twenty-and-change guy could be, Will's sibling Tom gave him a quick smile. "Yo. Owen."

"Hey, Tom." Owen smiled back, because Tom wasn't the type to take conversation into any uncomfortable territory. He wasn't likely to ask about the fire or about Jerry or about when Owen expected to be back on the job at the station. "How about those Raiders?" he added anyway, just to direct the conversation into a nonloaded area.

The other man groaned. "Did you have to bring that up?" he asked, his expression pained.

Owen did a quick mental review. It was early in the season, but the team was doing about as expected. "What's the matter? Did you make a bad bet with someone on last week's game?"

"This week's game," Tom mumbled. "I have tickets."

"And you have to work?"

"And I have a girlfriend," the other man said with a sigh.

"Oh," Owen answered, amused. "She doesn't like football?"

Tom slid lower onto the cushions, as if misery was yanking at his ankles. "At the moment, she doesn't like me."

"Sorry to hear that."

"Yeah," Tom said morosely, his gaze going distant. Then he jerked upright. "Wait, wait. Who's that?"

"Huh?" Owen looked in the same direction. "Who's what?"

"Oh, baby. The world is looking up. Chic-lookin' dark-haired chick just flitted into the kitchen. She has a very, *very* cute butt, and maybe Mr. Tom can find a new seatmate for Sunday's game."

Owen reminded himself that Tom was just acting his age and gender. It didn't help. "Was she wearing jeans and a red sweater?"

Tom's grin was appreciative. "*Tight* jeans, and—"

"She's with me," Owen growled.

"Oh." The younger man's smile died. "Sorry. No disrespect and all that."

"Fine."

Tom cast another speculative look toward the kitchen. "Except—"

"*Taken.*" Guilt at the claim bounced right off him. "Irrevocably taken."

"I got that," Tom said, "the minute your expression turned all ugly."

Ugly? Owen tried smoothing out his face.

"I just wondered if maybe she could introduce me to someone. I've still got those tickets."

"So you and your girlfriend…?"

"Gretchen." Tom turned morose again.

"Who am I fooling? I don't want to meet anyone else. I don't want to go with anyone but her to the game."

"Then you better make up with her or give away those tickets."

"Yeah." He glanced over at Owen. "I fell for her the minute I saw her. I was at this friend's birthday party and Gretchen walked toward me. I didn't have some perfect-girl image in my head. You know, this tall, or this colored hair, nothing like that. But here comes this girl and she tucks her hair behind her ears and her eye catches mine and I step closer and…well, she just smelled right, you know?"

"Sort of," Owen answered. He was such a liar. That's how it had been with Izzy. She'd walked up to him, put out her hand, and it had been just like Tom and Gretchen. It had just been right.

Or at least he'd thought so.

"Who could believe in love at first sight?" Tom continued, shaking his head. "But it happened to me."

That's not what had happened to Owen! It had been right, but right for the moment, right for the weekend, but not right for…right for… Damn! This was exactly the kind of conversation he didn't want to be having with Tom *or* with himself.

"Why don't you phone Gretchen?" he suggested. "See if you can get back in her good graces?"

Tom brightened. "You think I should do that?"

"Yeah. Find a nice private corner and

give her a call." And let me return to my peace and quiet.

To his relief, Tom thanked him for the advice and wandered off. Owen was alone again, alone with thoughts that wanted to wander again toward Izzy and rightness, but he refused to let them. A little kid toddled by with a small car in hand, and he allowed his casted wrist to be used as a roadway.

"There you are!" a voice called out.

He and the kid both jumped, then looked at Emily. She was smiling at the little guy. "Your mom's looking for you," she said. "She has a cup of pretzels for you."

A plaster roadway was no match for pretzels, apparently. The toddler hurried off and Emily sat in the place previously occupied by Tom. "I'm sorry we've been ignoring you."

"No problem." He couldn't be impolite and say it was what he'd been hoping for, could he? With a gesture, he indicated the hustle and bustle as people moved in and about the room. "I'm enjoying the chaos."

Emily smiled. "It terrified me at first. I was an only child, and the first couple of times I found myself at a Dailey clan event I was overwhelmed."

Maybe that was why Izzy had integrated so well into this party atmosphere, leaving him as the solo man on the sofa. Coming from a large family like this, she was likely accustomed to the commotion. Emily looked in fine form herself.

"You're good with it now, though," he said, tilting his head. "You look very good with it." Both Emily and Will shone with the same light he'd noticed beaming from them in Vegas. "You and Will."

"Yes." Just then, the man in question passed through the room and her gaze followed him. As if he felt it, he suddenly pivoted, walking backward while he shared a look with his wife. He gave her an intimate smile, then exited the room, causing Emily to turn back to Owen. "And you and Izzy?"

"Can we talk about something else?"

Her brows rose. "Uh, sure. How about those Raiders?"

"Tom has tickets to Sunday's game, I know that."

"But he's on temporary outs with Gretchen," Emily answered.

"Yeah. But I think he's on the phone over

there…" Owen turned to indicate the corner where—

Where Izzy stood, her shoulder leaning against the wall, her cell phone at her ear. He swore he could read her lips, and on that smiling mouth was the name of yet another hash mark for the "Male Callers" category. "Who is John?" Owen demanded.

"What?" Emily asked.

He couldn't stop himself. "Who is John—and Greg and David and Brad? There's likely more, because that damn phone of hers is ringing all the time."

"Am I the only one who thinks she needs to get a little more varied with the ring tone? Aren't you sick of 'Bohemian Rhapsody'?"

Okay, he knew he shouldn't press it. He was, after all, the one who wanted to not talk about Izzy. "Emily," he heard himself say anyway. "The woman takes more phone calls in a day than the department takes training runs in a year."

Emily laughed. "Yeah. You must be *really* sick of 'Bohemian Rhapsody.'"

"I thought they were calling regarding work, and then I thought they must be that large family of hers checking up on her, but she says they're all friends."

"They're not her family, that's for sure."

"Huh?"

Emily glanced over at Izzy, still chatting in the corner. "They forget she exists most of the time, I think."

"What are you talking about? She said she comes from this big Italian family. She implied they were the close-knit group you immediately think of when—" He broke off, frowning at Emily's compressed lips and shaking head. "They're not close-knit?"

"Not with Izzy. Maybe I shouldn't tell you…"

"Maybe you should," he insisted. "What's the deal?"

"Izzy won't thank you for feeling sorry for her…"

"I know how unpleasant it is to be felt sorry for. Don't worry about that. Just spill it, Emily."

"She's adopted." Emily darted a glance at Izzy and lowered her voice.

Owen had to lean closer to hear her over the hubbub in the house. "And?"

"And her parents quickly lost interest in having an infant. I think it was a passing phase, they fancied the idea of a child, but they run a tour agency—"

"She said that. Global excursions, particularly to Europe."

"Right, and they discovered that a baby put a crimp in their business plan. So they shuffled her around to various relatives, moving her from one Cavaletti to another to another. I don't think she stayed anyplace for more than a year or two."

Izzy. He tried imagining her circumstances. "Didn't anyone think that was cruel?"

"I don't know what they thought. I only know they let Izzy live with a succession of mostly maiden aunts and elderly widows. I think twice in her life she spent summers with families with kids. In essence, she raised herself."

Oh, Izzy.

"So instead of counting on the Cavalettis, she's made a family of friends for herself all over the country."

"The ones who hold on to her stuff," Owen said.

"Yeah. You know about that?"

"Boxes have been showing up at my place."

"Oops." Emily looked like she was biting back a smile. "I might be guilty of, um, letting it slip out that she's had a change in circumstance."

"It's making her crazy, having all her things showing up."

Emily's head tilted and her eyes narrowed. "Is it making *you* crazy?"

"No." *Izzy* was making him crazy—her

scent, her mouth, the memories of the two of them in bed—but not those cartons that kept arriving on the doorstep.

"Izzy's good at getting people to like her," Emily said.

"Probably because of all that moving around she had to do," Owen surmised.

"Probably," Emily agreed. "But I'm not sure she allows herself to depend on anyone, in case they disappoint her like her parents and relatives."

From the corner of his eye, he saw Izzy move past the couch and out of the room, her phone no longer in evidence. "She has so much," he murmured. "Beauty, brains, charm out the wazoo—"

"But no trust," Emily interjected, pushing to a stand. "I don't know that she can believe that anyone will make a lasting place for her in their life."

Owen wasn't, that was sure.

Though he shouldn't feel guilty over it, because that was the way both of them wanted it. She'd made that clear the day she'd run from him in Las Vegas. His runaway bride was back, but it was only to end their marriage.

Chapter Nine

Izzy was using her foot to shove the latest delivery away from the front door when Owen hobbled down the stairs. His eyebrows rose. "Another box?"

Heat crawled up her neck. "Somehow this address got out. Blasted e-mail loops."

"How many is that now?" he asked, sitting on one of the steps.

"Nine." She kicked at it, moving it just an inch or two. What was in this one? She couldn't remember. "I should just take them all straight to the Salvation Army."

"And lose your Louisa May Alcott books? Why would you do that?"

Izzy waved her hand. "All that happy family/happy romance was the stuff of childhood fantasy. I'm grown-up now." She knew the score and knew the difference between what a child longed for and what an adult could depend on. She glanced over at Owen, still aware of the embarrassed heat of her face. "I'm sorry for the inconvenience."

"Not inconvenient for me. You can store them in the garage, if you want. Indefinitely."

Indefinitely. But there was a definite

between them, a definite end date to this interlude. To their marriage. She snuck another look at him and noticed how tired he looked. Not sleeping again, she figured. His gaze was fixed, unseeing, on the shelving in the living room that held the vintage firefighter memorabilia.

And that reminded her…

"Say," she said, giving the box one last push with her foot so it was out of the way of the door. "How about we go for a drive? You can show me all the Paxton, California, scenic locations."

They could both use a diversion. She certainly wanted to think about something other than the belongings that were catching up with her. She had to be ready to leave at a moment's notice; it had always been that way for her, and too many things would only make it harder when she had to pick up and go.

Shoving the thought away, she noted the remote expression on Owen's face and the shadows under his eyes. He needed a change of place, too. "Let's get out of here, Owen."

"You'll have to play chauffeur," he reminded her.

She slapped on a grin, trying to lighten both their moods. "There's nothing I like better than to drive a man…crazy."

A smile ghosted over his mouth as he got to his feet. "You've got it down pat, sweetheart."

Heat washed over her again, across her face and down her body so that her skin felt too tight beneath her jeans and sweater. That night in his bed had been an aberration, but that didn't stop her from remembering every moment of it, from the first sure thrust of his tongue to the gentle withdrawal of his erection from the still-pulsing liquid center of her body.

She cleared her throat. "I could use some fresh air," she murmured.

"Won't help," he offered. "Last night I opened my window and stuck my whole head out and it didn't erase any thoughts from my brain or take my temperature down a single degree."

Oh, and as if that little comment cooled *her* off. She ignored him as she brushed past on her way to retrieve her purse. His low laugh was as good as a touch, though. It ruffled through her hair and traced like a fingertip down her spine.

Bad man.

Being closed up in his SUV didn't help matters much. Yes, they each had their own bucket seat, but this close she could smell his shampoo and see the strength of his long legs from the corner of her eye. Forcing her attention to the road, she said, "Where to?"

He directed her to his elementary school first. It was a typical, somewhat sprawling, suburban public school, with handpainted notices about the upcoming Fun Run and Halloween Festival taped to the surrounding fence. It was Saturday, so the fields were full of knee-socked little kids playing soccer. They moved about the grass in huddles and she and Owen idly watched their antics for a few minutes from the parking lot.

"So you spent kindergarten through fifth grade here?" she asked.

"Yep. Then I went to the junior high that's down the road and the high school beyond there. Go Paxton Panthers."

"I'll bet you were a jock."

"My mom already told you. In high school I played football and ran track. But I was a smart jock, remember? Salutatorian."

"And modest, too," she teased.

He reached over and yanked on the ends of her hair. "Hey, when a guy doesn't have his full mobility he's got to keep his ego pumped."

"Ah." She trained her gaze out the window, not daring to look at him. "So that's what you call it."

He groaned. "You're heading into dangerous territory, pretty girl."

She shook her head. "I wasn't one, you know. I wasn't a jock and I wasn't pretty, either. I was brainy and I wore glasses and I was the kind of girl the guys never looked at twice."

"Now that's a lie."

"Really."

"You just never caught the guys looking at you. I noticed that about the bookworms. They should have glanced up from the page a time or two."

Izzy glanced over at him now. Big mistake. That…that *thing* that had been between them from the first moment in Las Vegas flared to life again. Her breath caught and her thigh muscles clenched, and she felt herself tremble as he reached over to play with her hair. His fingertips brushed the rim of her ear as he tucked some strands behind it, then toyed with the small gold ring there.

"You're so damn pretty now, Isabella," he said.

They both moved at once, each leaning toward the other. Her mouth tingled, in anticipation of his kiss. "Damn pretty," he said again, his breath washing over her lips.

Thunk!

They started, and straightening, Izzy saw a soccer ball roll off the hood of the car. "Whoa," she said.

"Wake-up call," he muttered.

Checking her watch, she turned the key in the ignition. "Where should we go next?" Someplace that wouldn't allow for that inconvenient intimacy to arise between them again. Those waters were dangerous.

"Let's check out the old homestead."

He directed her through suburban streets

with green lawns and mature trees that had leaves just turning to autumn's colors. There were kids on the sidewalks on bicycles and people walking dogs, and if she could have put it all in a bubble with little white flakes, it would have made a perfect snow globe.

She sighed as he indicated a house on a corner with wraparound grass and large trees anchoring each end. "You actually grew up there?"

"I actually grew up there."

"But your family lives in San Francisco now."

"After Bryce graduated from high school, Mom and Dad moved into the city. But before that, we were right here, doing the whole small-town thing."

Izzy sighed again. Add seven boy cousins

and she would have been in heaven in such an environment. "Is that a treehouse?"

"Yep. We even rigged a bucket on the end of a rope so that we could haul up snacks that my mom would bring out to us. On Halloween, once we were past the age of trick-or-treating, we put up ghosts and ghouls inside and made our buddies pay us a quarter to go through it."

"Oh, Owen." She smiled over at him. "It must have been great."

"Yeah." He shrugged. "But the city has its pluses, too. If I go to work for the family company, I'll probably move there to avoid a long commute."

"You're still considering that?"

He hedged. "I'm reading all those boring reports."

"But—"

"I remember you commenting a couple of days ago it wasn't your business," he said, scowling.

"Yes, but—"

"And it *isn't* your business, Izzy."

She scowled back. Fine, then. They might not have a discussion about what he should do, but she still had a little demonstration up her sleeve. With a twist of her wrist, she restarted the car.

"Where now?" he asked.

"I'll head downtown. See what's up."

The Paxton "downtown" was three blocks of small shops and restaurants with the city administration building and the central fire station at the northern end. As they neared the main thoroughfare, they found that the road was barricaded and people were lining the sidewalks.

"What's going on?" Owen asked aloud.

He'd still been ignoring the local newspaper, but she hadn't. "Parade," she answered. She swung into the parking lot of a bank, digging into her purse to give the attending Boy Scout the five bucks the troop was charging for a prime location. Just as the first marching band passed them, she was turning off the engine and setting the emergency brake.

She snuck a look to her right. Owen had gone expressionless again, his face betraying nothing as the groups marched past. There was the junior high jazz band playing something—pretty badly—from their places in the back of a pickup. Tiny gymnasts came next, in spangled leotards and carrying a banner that read "Paxton Pixies." Next up was the obligatory horse riders in flashy chaps and silver-studded finery, their animals' hides gleaming.

Then a mixed group of Boy Scouts and Girl Scouts, carrying a sign:

Paxton Fire Department: 100 Years of Service
100 Times That Many Thanks from Paxton Citizens!

The crowds on the sidewalk cheered, then cheered louder as a fire-engine-red fire engine slowly rolled down the street. Firefighters, including Will, Izzy noted, leaned out of the vehicle, throwing candy at the parade watchers.

"Let's go," Owen ground out.

"Don't you want to enjoy—"

"For God's sake, Izzy, give me some credit," he said. "I know what you're trying to do. But surely you realize I didn't do the job for the parades."

"Why did you do the job?" She cleared her throat. "Why do you do the job?"

He opened his mouth. Closed it. Opened it again. Then he ran his hand through his hair. "I don't know, damn it. I don't know the why of anything anymore."

The words tore at her heart. Dangerous territory, indeed. She twisted the key in the ignition and blinked away the sting of tears in her eyes before backing up and leaving the parking lot. Though she was pretty sure no matter how many miles they put between themselves and this place, there was no getting away from the uncertainty he'd just shared.

Owen didn't protest when Izzy made another stop before returning to his place. Privacy wasn't what the two of them should risk right now. He was equal parts angry and horny, and she'd been rubbing against him in both the right and wrong ways all morning.

They were either going to get into a full-fledged fight or they were going to get into bed. Neither was a good idea, and before meeting Izzy he would have thought he had enough control over himself to make sure what he didn't want didn't happen.

But she added points to his blood pressure

just by the way she looked in a pair of old jeans and black boots.

And he was the one who prided himself on his calm demeanor and his cool under pressure.

"I thought we could have some lunch," she said, pulling into a parking space of the lot beside a small Italian restaurant. "Every time I drive past this place the smell makes my taste buds start crying."

It did smell delicious, he had to admit as he limped into the restaurant, using the cane that it still annoyed him to be relying upon. He knew the food tasted just as good as it smelled; he'd been there a time or two with a date, though he decided against admitting to that. Frankly, when he slid into the booth opposite the woman he'd married, he couldn't picture any other woman's face across the table.

They both ordered. When the waiter was gone, she toyed with the stem of her water goblet. "Owen…"

His attention was focused on her fingertip, the one that was ringing the base of the glass. He remembered her small fingers caressing his chest, the way they stroked the back of her hand against his jaw, how she'd gripped the ends of his hair as she rode him in sweet, cowgirl style.

God, he'd loved to see her do that again, while still wearing those shiny black boots…

"Owen?"

He blinked, bringing himself back to the moment. Oh. Right. Lunch.

"What?" The word came out rough.

She blinked, blushed. "About earlier… about at the parade…"

His temper shot up again. "Damn it, Izzy—"

"I wanted to say I'm sorry." She reached across the table and touched his hand with those seductive fingertips of hers. "You were right, I was wrong. I had no business putting that in your face or asking you any kind of questions at all."

Her apology deflated him. He slumped against the back of the banquette. "Izzy…" Without a clue where to go next, he let the word die.

She curled her fingers around his and tightened them. "Don't be mad."

He swallowed his silent groan. Mad might be better. But this, her touch, her big, brown eyes, they only made him have other kinds of feelings, ones that were just as hot, but even more dangerous than anger. "I'm not mad," he said, slipping his hand away from hers and curling his fingers into a fist that he placed on his thigh.

Away from temptation.

Their food arrived, and he applied himself to his meal, aware of the awkward silence between them. He wasn't going to break it. If anger wasn't in the air, awkward would do just as well. He would nurture anything that would keep the distance between them.

As they finished the food on their plates, the waitstaff arranged tables nearby, creating a long stretch that was soon filled by what appeared to be multiple generations of one family. One large, Italian family.

Dark hair, dark eyes, a plethora of people whose looks reminded him of Izzy's.

The group attracted her attention, as well. As she pushed her nearly empty plate to the side, she watched them pass around menus and swap chairs. A small child began to wail and was instantly picked up by an older lady who could have been its grandmother or great-grandmother. She unearthed a package of crackers from somewhere, and the child leaned against the lady's big bosom and contentedly munched, tears drying. Two older youngsters started a loud squabble until a man—their father?—reached over and cuffed them lightly on the tops of their heads.

Izzy looked back at Owen and their eyes met. They both smiled. "Look familiar?" he asked.

Her smiled died as a strange expression passed over her face. She hesitated, then stole another glance at the family next door. "Oh, uh, sure. The Cavalettis are like that. Big, happy, everybody with a place at the table."

Owen stilled, his fork halfway to his mouth. He'd meant that the family resembled Izzy in appearance, not that her family had been a loving, happy group like this one. From what Emily had implied, that hadn't been the case at all. In fact, Izzy had spent most of her childhood on her own.

"There's nothing better than feeling part of a close-knit clan," she continued.

Which, Owen realized with a jolt, explained why *Eight Cousins* had been her favorite childhood book. That had been her fantasy as a kid. A big, happy clan that made room for every member at the table. He laid his fork on his plate, his appetite gone, as he thought of how lonely she must have been and how she was still telling herself stories to fill up that old void in her life.

"Izzy," he said. "Isabella." He reached across the table to find her hand.

It curled in his, small and delicate, and something filled his chest, making it hard to breathe. He looked down at her ring finger, remembered sliding that narrow gold band down the short slender length, and he replayed the moment in his head, recapturing just how he'd felt under the disco lights at the Elvis Luvs U Wedding Chapel.

A trio of emotions had bubbled inside him. Anticipation, exhilaration and a sense of inevitability that he'd not even attempted to escape. He'd not wanted to hesitate; he'd only wanted to hold her.

He rubbed his thumb over her knuckles. Her eyes met his and he could see her pupils widen. He slid the pad of his thumb between her fingers, stroking over the silky inner skin. Her breath was moving faster, and he could see her breasts rising and falling beneath her sweater. His pulse started to throb in time with the movement.

Anger hadn't helped. The awkwardness between them was gone. That strong sexual pull was back, and he didn't think he had a chance of keeping distant from her now.

"Remember what I said about fresh air not helping?" he asked softly.

Her nostrils flared and she nodded.

Maybe if she wasn't so beautiful, he thought. Maybe if he didn't remember that the silken texture of the inner surface of her fingers exactly matched that of the inner surface of her thighs. But he really thought it was that independent exterior of hers that he now knew protected such a vulnerable core that got to him.

She was bravado and beauty and loneliness and…lust.

Yeah, like him, she felt that, too.

He could see it in the flush of her face and the way her tongue slipped out to wet her lips. Any second thought he might have had evaporated as he stared at her plush, tempting mouth. Her throat moved as she swallowed.

"Owen…?" she whispered.

"Yeah?"

"The fresh air didn't help me, either."

His hand tightened on hers. Then he smiled and released her fingers so he could reach for his wallet. He threw some bills on the table. "Let's go home."

As he slowly limped toward the door, leaning on his cane, he decided they both deserved what pleasure they could find together. Yeah, it might be temporary, but they were grown-ups. Each of them had their reasons for agreeing to more human contact. Izzy, because she lived her foot-loose lifestyle that likely made connections few and far between. And him, because of that parade. Because—

"Owen."

He halted, looking toward the sound of the voice. In the booth he was passing, a man rose. "Mick," Owen answered. He shifted the cane to his casted hand so he could meet the grip of his captain, Mick Hanson.

"It's good to see you," Mick said.

"You, too." Even though Owen felt guilty as hell for the way he'd been ducking the other man's calls in the past couple of weeks, he managed a smile that he directed to everyone in the booth. He recognized Mick's two school-age kids, Jane and Lee, as well as the young woman who'd been their babysitter since Mick's wife died five years before.

He remembered Kayla as a pretty college coed, but now he could see that she'd turned into a very attractive woman. For a second, Owen wondered if Mick had noticed that, too, though something told him it was unlikely.

"Nice to see you kids," he said, then he smiled at the woman. "And I like the new haircut, Kayla."

Mick's head whipped toward the babysitter. "You have a new haircut? Since when?"

Jane rolled her eyes in the way of daughters everywhere. "Since two weeks ago, Daddy."

"Oh." Frowning, Mick returned his attention to Owen. "I'm glad I ran into you. You need to come by the station this afternoon."

"No." He tried softening his instant refusal, even as his gaze strayed toward the restaurant's front door where Izzy was hovering. "I have a friend. We have plans…."

"Bring the friend. Postpone the plans," Mick insisted. "There are people who need to see you."

"But…"

"Bring the friend," Mick said again, his tone of voice brooking no argument. "Postpone the plans."

Sighing, Owen nodded, even though he realized that what he needed distance from, more than Izzy, more than anything, was what his boss had just ordered him to do.

Chapter Ten

Izzy told herself she was glad that Owen wanted to stop by the fire station after lunch. Bryce had said he needed to visit his co-workers, and apparently his captain thought the same thing. Even better, it gave her head a chance to take control over her hormones. They'd been a short car ride away from ending up in bed again, and that would have been a big mistake.

They were nothing more than casual friends, when it came right down to it. And you didn't need to read a lot of books or listen to therapists on afternoon TV to know that turning casual into sexual opened up a can of worms. Sort of like marrying someone after a three-day acquaintance.

"Pull in over there," Owen said, indicating a space in a parking area between the main fire station and the city's municipal building.

"It looks new," Izzy observed, studying the attractive stucco building with its simple landscaping and three wide bays for emergency vehicles. Bunches of balloons waved here and there in the breeze, and the double front doors were flung wide open.

"It is new," Owen said. "A recent bond issue provided the money. That's why there's an open house today. Not only because it's the hundredth anniversary of the department, but also to give the public a chance to tour the facilities."

He didn't appear eager to visit himself, however. As they watched people wander in and out of the building, he stayed glued to his seat. Then, with a sigh, he reached for the door handle. "You ready?"

Um, no. Because watching him wage this little war with himself wasn't helping her head take control of the situation. Now her heart was getting involved, too, aching a little to see how hard it was for him to face the place and the people he'd worked with.

Each step across the asphalt only served to tighten her nerves. She'd asked him, while they were watching the parade, why he was a firefighter. He'd answered, *"I don't know, damn it. I don't know the why of anything anymore."*

The man was second-guessing how he'd spent the past years of his life and what he was going to do with the next ones. She couldn't imagine, just from the way Bryce had reacted, that getting into the family business was something that would suit Owen. And she could easily see him bumping heads with the elder Mr. Marston on a daily basis.

Would that be as satisfying as the important work of a first responder?

She glanced around, realizing he wasn't beside her any longer. Instead of walking up the path that led to the front door of the facility, Owen was halted at the bottom of it, his jaw set, his expression grim. Her heart squeezed again and she retraced her steps.

"Owen?" She touched the back of his hand.

He shook himself and gripped his cane tighter. "Let's go in," he said, starting forward.

"All right." Without thinking twice about it, she wove her fingers with those of his sticking out of the cast. "Let's go in."

Of course that gesture wasn't casual. Maybe it appeared friendly, though, because as they breached the threshold to the fire station, the first person they ran into by the front desk—Will—didn't even blink to see them so connected.

"Owen." He grinned, but didn't reach out for the customary handshake.

She wondered about that for a second, until she realized that Owen wasn't stretching his palm toward his friend, either. No, he was still holding on to his cane and Izzy like life-lines.

He didn't even notice, she thought, glancing over. She didn't think he noticed Will, either, because his attention was focused exclusively on an enlarged photo-graph set up on an easel at the far corner of the building's foyer.

A photograph of Jerry Palmer.

There was a massive pile of flowers and stuffed animals and hand-lettered notes at the foot of the easel. As they watched, a boy, accompanied by his mother, placed a bear dressed in a firefighter's uniform beside a mass of autumn-colored chrysanthemums.

The child turned, and his gaze snagged on Owen. "Mom!" he said in a loud voice, tugging at her sleeve so he could tow her in their direction. "Look, it's Mr. Marston."

The boy's mother was blond and shapely, in cropped jeans, sneakers and a V-necked T-shirt that revealed a little too much cleavage, if Izzy were asked to offer an opinion. Her glossy mouth turned up in a delighted smile as she and the boy surged forward.

"Owen!" she said, reaching out both hands.

Oh, so *now* he let go of his wife and allowed the blond cutie to squeeze his fingers. "I'm so glad to see that you're on the mend," she said, beaming.

He smiled back, though it did look a tad automatic. "Better every day," he said, and then he reached out to ruffle the boy's hair. "And thanks for the get-well card you sent, Ryan. The licorice, too."

The kid glanced up at his mom and then back at his apparent hero. "It was Mom's idea. *I* wanted to lend you my game system, but she said with your broken arm and all…"

Owen held up his cast. "Just the wrist, but it does seriously affect my *Halo* score."

"Can I sign it?" Ryan asked, looking at the bright blue plaster with the envy only a kid could have for such a device. "You don't have any signatures. You're supposed to have people write their names and stuff."

"I suppose you're right." Owen put on another of those forced-looking smiles. "Why don't you be the first?"

The boy's grin split his face. "Mom, do you have a pen?"

She shook her head, and then Will

stepped in. "Ryan, come with me and we'll rustle up a marker."

The two took off, leaving Izzy and Owen and Ryan's mom, who for the first time seemed to notice someone other than Izzy's husband. Her gaze ran over Izzy, from the top of her hair to the heels of her boots.

Straightening her spine a little, Izzy was pleased that while her jeans were on the battered side, her black boots were new and oh-so-much chicer than the other woman's soccer-mom footwear. Okay, Izzy wasn't all that proud of herself for the thought, but the blonde was, well, blond. And busty.

The busty blonde held out her hand to Izzy. "I'm sorry, I didn't catch your name. I'm Alicia Ayers."

Alliterative Alicia wasn't wearing a

wedding band. "Izzy Cavaletti," she said, shaking hands.

"I know Owen because, well, he saved our lives."

"Did he?" Izzy turned to look at the man in question, who had been hailed by another firefighter and was slightly turned away.

"Ryan and I were in a rollover car accident a few months back. We landed upside down in a ditch and the first to arrive on scene were Owen and Jerry Palmer." Her pretty mouth turned down. "They stayed with us and kept us calm until the right kind of equipment was brought to pry us out."

"I'm glad you were both okay."

"Me, too." The blonde's gaze darted to Owen again. "We've been friends ever since. I'm divorced, and Ryan has taken a real shine to Owen."

"I'll bet." And Izzy bet that Ryan wasn't the only one who had taken a shine to the man who was now extending his cast for the boy to sign. She looked back at the divorcée, whose gaze was resting fondly on the—boy?—man? "Owen is surely easy to, um, like."

"So…" The other woman looked back at Izzy, paused, then shrugged, as if she'd lost a debate with herself. "How are you two acquainted?"

Izzy glanced at Owen again. Someone had pulled up a chair for him so he could get off his feet. He had his cast propped on his knees and was watching while the youngster drew a picture along the plaster.

His expression was open, easier than it had been since she'd come to Paxton and found him lying in the hospital bed.

It reminded her of how he'd struck her in Las Vegas. A big man with a big smile, friendly and confident enough not to hesitate to greet his best friend's girl's best friend. He hadn't hesitated to dance with her, kiss her, make her crush on him just a little, and just enough to get her to go ahead and say "I do" when Elvis stood before them with his guitar strapped across his chest and a Bible in his hand.

So Izzy didn't hesitate now. Fully aware she could claim a casual friendship with him, or even "home health worker" status like she had with Mr. Marston, she instead looked the pretty divorced woman right in the eye and said, "I'm his wife."

Hey, it was only the truth, wasn't it?

The woman's baby blues flared wide and then Izzy felt the heat of a stare on her backside. Uh-oh. She didn't think Owen was admiring her bottom, not at the moment anyway. He was more likely aghast at how she'd just complicated his romantic life with Alicia.

But had Cutie Pie been making him grilled-cheese-and-tomato sandwiches? Had she been pouring his milk over ice? Had she spent a night in his bed and—

Oh. She didn't want to go there. She didn't want to know if the woman's gratitude had been expressed in ways other than greeting cards and candy.

"Isabella?" The low note in Owen's voice did not spook her. It did not.

She just had a sudden hankering for some of those refreshments she saw stacked on a table across the foyer. "Excuse me," she said, with a polite smile for the divorcée. Owen she didn't dare look at. "I'll be back in a few minutes."

Just as soon as she got her emotions under control. First it was lust and now it was jealousy. Goodness. She needed to work on her perspective. She scurried away, heading for the bin of bottled water. As she reached for one, her hand collided with that of someone else.

"Oops," she said, and looked into the face of another woman. Younger than Alicia. Younger than Izzy. She had red-rimmed eyes, and the tip of her nose was pink. Her belly stuck out like a beach ball.

And Izzy was assaulted by yet more emotions as she surmised the identification of the very pregnant person with whom she was playing tug of war with a bottle of water. Her eyes pricked in sympathy and her stomach rolled as she thought back to the tragic fire.

This had to be Ellie Palmer. Jerry's widow.

Izzy's head had no control over the knowledge that speared straight into her heart. This young woman had lost her husband that night, just as Izzy could have lost hers.

Owen looked after the woman running away from him, for a moment distracted by the upside-down heart shape of her cute, denim-covered butt. And Izzy thought boys hadn't noticed her in high school. That might only be because she wasn't looking behind her as she walked off.

"So, you're married?"

Alicia's voice jerked his attention her way. "Uh…"

"You never mentioned it." Two lines appeared between her brows, and the sharpness in her voice had her son glancing up from the dragon/tiger/eagle—it could have been any or all—he was penning on Owen's cast.

"It's sort of a recent thing."

She was still frowning. "You didn't strike me as a man interested in marriage."

Funny, because he'd never thought about the marriage deal one way or another. His parents had a great one, and he'd probably taken it for granted, because he hadn't considered how he would achieve such a partnership like that for himself. It wasn't that he was against it, exactly, but…

Alicia was right, before he hit Las Vegas and looked in the velvet-brown eyes of one Isabella Cavaletti, he hadn't thought about himself and marriage at all. But then he'd met her, touched her, smiled into her eyes, and there had been that connection. They'd instantly clicked in a physical way, and then there was their mutual misheard lyrics idiosyncrasy—"Hold me closer, Tony Danza." Which of course sounded like a damn stupid reason to wed a woman, but there he'd been, at the altar, a big ol' contented grin on his face.

"There!" Ryan crowed, straightening from the work he was doing on Owen's cast.

Owen looked down at the creature crawling across the plaster. "Looks great. Thank you."

The boy grinned. "It's your warrior. With your arm broken and your legs not one hundred percent, this guy'll step up and do your battles for you."

"Hey, I appreciate it." Owen smiled, because the kid made him think of Bryce. And looking at the kid's towhead, it made him think of…himself.

Good God. It made him think of himself as a father. Damn. There was a completely new, completely baffling idea. A boy like Ryan. A mother, like…

Like…

His gaze lifted. A mother not like Alicia. And not that there was anything wrong with her. She was beautiful and a devoted mom. But when he thought about the next generation, his next generation, he could only think of one woman…

Hell. He was thinking of Izzy, of course.

And he needed to find her. Be near her. Now.

With a gentle hand, he ruffled Ryan's hair. "Thanks so much for what you drew." His gaze lifted to Alicia. "Thanks so much for…"

He broke off. Because he couldn't articulate what she'd demonstrated. It wasn't fully formed in his mind, not yet. It still was a vague, amorphous…something.

Alicia was looking at him, her mouth quirked in a bemused smile. "Well, congratulations on your marriage," she said. She looked over his shoulder and he glanced back, seeing that her gaze had drifted to the enlarged photo of Jerry. "And remember that we shouldn't waste time with anything but happy."

The happy that the dead man couldn't experience anymore.

On that, Owen's upbeat mood surge disappeared. But not the need to find Izzy. She was his means to getting home, he told himself. That's why he needed her more than ever.

Pushing up from the chair he was in, he accepted the cane that Ryan immediately handed him. "Thanks, pal," he said, his right hand closing over the handle. He gave the kid a smile that felt as forced as he was sure it appeared.

Looking around the small crowd in the foyer, he saw Izzy's dark head. Focusing his gaze there, he threaded through the people, touching the back of her shoulder once he reached her.

She turned. There were tears in her eyes.

"Sweetheart." He frowned, his hand trailing down her arm. Concern for her added to his own low mood. "What's the matter?"

Izzy shifted so that he could see she'd been conversing with another young woman. Oh. Oh, God.

Ellie Palmer.

Images slammed into him again. Fractured pictures from that night and from his recurrent nightmare. He smelled smoke and he heard shouts and the gnawing, crunching sound that flames made as they ate at a structure. His vision dimmed and it was only Jerry's grin he could see, flashing on and off like the strobe on top of the fire engine.

"Owen. *Owen*. Are you okay?"

He blinked, startled to find himself outside the station and limping across the parking lot toward his car. Izzy had her hand in the crook of his elbow, above his cast, and was leading him like a blind man.

Embarrassment shot through him. He stumbled, and Izzy clutched tighter, keeping him upright.

"Are you okay?" she asked again.

He felt like such an idiot, he couldn't look at her. "I'm fine," he managed to get out. "Just fine."

"You're not," she answered, unlocking the passenger door for him. "And I know it. So don't even try the macho baloney with me."

He climbed into the car instead of answering. Once she was in her seat, she shut her door then started the car and pulled out of the parking spot. "I thought I was going to lose it, too, when I first realized it was her," Izzy said softly.

He kept staring out the window.

"Then I decided that my little breakdown wasn't going to help. So we talked about the baby. It's a boy. She's going to name him Alexander Gerald Palmer. Alexander is the name of Jerry's dad."

Owen's hand tightened on the crook of his cane until his knuckles were white. He couldn't think of one damn thing to say.

"She and Jerry painted the nursery with pale-blue and yellow stripes. It's all ready for the baby."

Jerry's baby. The baby he would never see.

"And—"

"Damn it, Izzy!" he burst out. Emotion broke over him again, like a cold, clammy sweat. "Do you think this is what I want to hear?"

"No," she answered, her voice quiet. "But I want to help, and your wall of silence isn't making things better, either. I know you're hurting, and I'd like to find some way to make it better."

Her words, her tone, took the fight out of him. It wasn't her fault. It was his, wasn't it? That night of the fire, he should have foreseen, he should have felt that things would go south. As Izzy drove, he ran everything he could remember through his head. It continued to be hazy in some places, but he forced every memory back that he could, from the first moment of the call until he'd felt the world cracking beneath his feet. How had it all gone so wrong?

He was barely aware that they'd made it home and that he and Izzy were slowly climbing the stairs to the bedroom. Still preoccupied with the past, he dropped down onto the edge of the bed. "I should be the one who's gone," he murmured, finally articulating the thought that had been hounding him since he woke up in the hospital.

Izzy sat on the mattress beside him. He looked into her eyes, their velvet darkness trained on his face, and for the first time spoke the words that had been sitting like acid in his belly for the last four weeks. "I would give anything to go back and have the one who is alive be Jerry."

She brushed her fingers through his hair, pushing it off his forehead. "I know," she whispered. "I know."

It was the exact right response, he realized. She didn't try talking him out of the feeling, she didn't try telling him that he should be happy he was alive, which he'd either told himself a hundred times or had heard from his family and friends. Izzy accepted his words, even seemed to understand them, and he couldn't begin to tell her how grateful he was for that.

Her fingers combed through his hair again and she leaned up to press a gentle kiss on his mouth. It was sweet, as understanding as her words, as soothing as her touch, but it ignited him all the same.

His good hand came around to the back of

her head to keep her mouth centered on his. He deepened the kiss, surging into the wet heat of her mouth. He needed this, too, her understanding and this powerful sexual connection of theirs.

"Izzy?" he murmured against her mouth.

"Yes." She was already pulling the tails of his shirt out of his jeans. The fabric slid against his belly, making him shudder. Her small fingers went to work on the buttons even as he tried yanking off her sweater with his one good hand.

Their frantic fumbling might have been funny, and under other circumstances they might have laughed, but seriousness lay over them like a blanket. It slowed their movements, too, so that when they finally were naked from the waist up, it seemed like it took a week for her to respond to the press of his hand on the smooth, hot skin of her back. When the hard tips of her nipples finally met his chest wall, they both gasped.

They collapsed onto the mattress, their mouths meeting, melding, the heat between them making it imperative that he get them out of their pants. His hand popped open the snap of her jeans and yanked down her zipper. A small triangle of cherry-red fabric distracted his purpose and he slid is hand beneath it—to find her already hot and wet and so soft that his fingers curled into her as he groaned his approval against her mouth.

She bucked against his hand, her torso twisting against his so that her nipples dragged through the hair on his chest. He slid another finger into her, filling her, and her hips jerked hard. His thumb easily found the center of her pleasure at the top of her flowered sex. He rolled over it, once, twice, while Izzy moaned into his mouth.

She grabbed his wrist. "Owen, stop. I'm…almost, I…don't…"

Yeah, she was almost there. He could feel it in the tension of her muscles and see it in the flush on her face. "But I do, Izzy," he said, continuing to stroke the sleek heat between her legs. "I do need this."

After the disastrous outcome of that fire, he needed to have control of something, and taking charge of her pleasure was calming the roil of emotions that had been churning in his gut all day. Drawing his mouth away from hers, he trailed it across her cheek, her ear, and then down her neck. She bowed into him, her body squeezing his invading fingers, her breath coming fast. He glanced up, their eyes met, and he watched the orgasm crash over her.

Still half-broken, in that moment Owen felt whole.

But there was more ahead. She wiggled out of her jeans, helped him with his and then they were together on the bed, their bodies moving in that dance that came to them so naturally.

He kissed her mouth, he buried his nose in the perfumed smoothness of her neck, he let her rock him into his own burst of pleasure and then into…peace.

That's what she offered, too, he realized.

He'd been able to tell her the darkest secret of his soul and she'd responded with the intimacy of her body. This is what marriage was about, he decided, as he watched her drift into sleep on the pillow beside him.

You shared it all, and the other person took you in. Your partner was your shelter when you needed that, was your peace when that was paramount, was in your corner no matter how unwinnable the fight.

This was what love was about.

And love was exactly what Owen Marston realized he felt for his wife.

Chapter Eleven

Izzy heard the uneven limp of Owen behind her. "What are you doing?" he asked.

She smiled to herself and continued through the door that led down the steps to the garage, a box in her arms. "I'm learning a new language while teaching myself tiddly winks."

"Okay, fine. Laugh at me." He sounded

out of sorts, but nowhere near the dark mood he'd been in after their visit to the fire station a few days before. This one was more of a boyish, it's-a-rainy-day-and-there's-nothing-to-do variety. He was walking better and his wrist was starting to itch beneath the plaster.

"He's bored," Izzy whispered to herself as she hitched the box higher in her hands and set it on one of the two towers she'd created. This latest carton had been delivered that morning, but she'd moved the others down here before. There were twelve altogether now, and at some point she was going to have to find a new storage spot for them. There were other tasks on her list first, however.

She climbed the steps only to find Owen

waiting for her at the top. Leaning on his cane, he wrapped his casted arm around her back and pulled her close for a kiss. With a little sigh, she melted against him. For better or worse—just like their marriage vows—they'd been sleeping together since the fire station visit.

"You got up too early this morning," he complained, nuzzling a sensitive spot below her jaw. His mouth skittered down her neck. "Let's go back to bed."

Goose bumps broke over her skin. Yes. They could go back to bed and she could pull him over her body just like warm covers and make the world go away. But no, today she had made plans that required looking the world in the eye.

Owen couldn't hide anymore, and she was

going to have to find a way to break that truth to him.

She broke out of his hold instead and tromped up the stairs toward the third level that housed the bedrooms. "Later," she said, looking down at him with a smile.

He groaned in mock frustration. "Isa-bellllla."

She laughed. He drew her name out like that when she did things to make him crazy, like order him to stay completely still while she inspected the heated skin of his chest…with her tongue.

Up in the room where she kept her things but no longer slept, she started folding the small pile of clean laundry on her bed. She didn't hear Owen until he spoke from the threshold of the door. "What are you doing?"

His brows were lowered and there was a frown on his face. "Izzy?"

She had no idea what he was talking about. She looked around the room. It was neat and clean, and her small suitcase, sitting open on top of the long dresser, was, as always, well organized. With a short pile of T-shirts in one hand, she crossed to it and tucked the clothes into the appropriate corner. "Is there something wrong?"

"Why are you packing?" he asked.

"Packing?" She frowned, then realized that he must never have peeked into the bedroom she'd slept in when she'd first arrived. "Oh. This is just…just how I live. Out of suitcases. I never put things in drawers."

He crossed the carpeting to sit on the end of her bed. His hand idly played with the small heap of not-yet-folded underthings a few inches away. She watched him toy with the delicate lace on a pair of just-washed thong panties that she vividly remembered him stripping off her one steamy night.

He'd parted her legs, then kneeled low so he could taste her there. "Sweet," he'd said, looking up. "Hot." She'd already been on fire, her nerve endings crackling and sparking like live wires after a storm.

But the storm had been yet to come. He'd bent down again, holding her knees wide so that he could keep her open as he tongued and tasted her there, coiling the desire inside her belly until it moved lower and lower and then spun out in a great frenzied whiplash of a release.

Now, she turned away from him so he

wouldn't see how affected she was just by him touching the clothes that weren't even on her body. That would tighten his hold on her, if he knew. And everything she'd been planning was about loosening the ties between them.

"Izzy, sweetheart."

"Hmm?"

"Look at me," he commanded.

If she refused, he'd make something out of that, too, so she whirled around and gave him a brilliant smile. "What?"

He was twirling a tiny pair of leopard-print panties on his forefinger. An unholy grin lit up his face. "These make me want to growl."

Heat shot up her face again and she stomped over to grab all the underwear, including the pair now dangling from his finger. She shoved the handful into an interior pocket of her suitcase. "There. All done. Now can we please leave behind the topic of my clothes?"

He shook his head, his grin dying. "I still think it's odd that you haven't unpacked the entire time you've been here."

"I told you. I always live out of my suitcase." It made it so much easier to move out and move on, a lesson she'd learned early. "If you don't keep your belongings close, you might inadvertently leave something of value behind."

There was a long pause. "Oh, Isabella," he finally said. "Sometimes you sucker punch me without even meaning to."

"I don't have a clue as to what you're

talking about." The way he was looking at her made her stomach jump up and down in a very unpleasant manner, she thought, frowning at him. "I've been traveling this way since childhood—"

"Exactly." He caught her hand and drew her close to him. "Let's talk about your traveling childhood."

"I don't have time for that."

He yanked on her hand, pulling her onto his lap. "Sure you do. I was talking to Emily a while back, and—"

"I need to go make lunch." Izzy struggled to get up, but his cast was pressed against her waist.

"We can have a late lunch. Or I can make lunch. Or we can go out to lunch. Let's forget about lunch altogether and talk."

"I've invited someone over." She bit her lip. She'd meant it to be a surprise, but that probably wasn't fair anyhow.

Owen groaned. "If you say it's my grandfather…"

"It's not."

"Are you sure? Because I know Granddad has been calling you, my lovely home health worker, for daily updates."

She smiled, because something about the older gentleman tickled her. He was loud and brash and absolutely devoted to his grandson. "And don't I cover for you every single time? I tell him you're napping or showering or—"

"Bryce said you once told Granddad I was behind a closed door with a *Playboy* magazine and couldn't be disturbed."

Her mouth fell open and she scrambled off his lap. "I did no such thing!"

Owen laughed. "Okay, then Bryce made that one up." He brightened. "Tell me it's my brother coming for lunch and I can think up some fitting way to pay him back. Like, you made brownies for dessert and now he doesn't get any."

"No, it's not Bryce, either," she said.

Something on her face must have warned him. He sobered, his gaze narrowing. "Who is it, Isabella?"

She retreated for the door, her fluttering heart joining the up-and-down movement of her stomach. "It's Jerry's wife. It's Ellie Palmer."

He stared at her.

"You didn't speak to her at all at the fire

station that day. You took one look at her and walked out. So she called yesterday to see…to see how you were." Izzy wiped her palms on her thighs. Her other attempts at interference hadn't worked, but this time it had to. "What could I say?"

"'Come over for lunch' doesn't seem the most natural first response." His expression was closed off and he'd crossed his arms over his chest. "But hey, whatever. I'll get out of the house and out of your hair so you two women can chat."

"No, no! You…you haven't been driving."

"Then it's about time that I do." He made to rise.

She leaped over to push him down by the shoulders. It was imperative he meet with Jerry's widow. It was the necessary final step in his healing process. Once he was emotionally whole again, Izzy could finally walk away from him.

The longer she put that off, the harder walking away would be for her. "Owen, you know you need to speak with Ellie."

"No, I don't."

"Even if just to tell her what you know about Jerry's last evening."

"I'm sure other people have told her all about that. We had enchiladas. Somebody at the station just loves to make enchiladas."

"You had another nightmare last night," she told him. "I think that means you've got to face—"

"Stay out of my head, Izzy." His voice was low and controlled. "Remember? We made that deal?"

"*If* I stayed out of your bed," she reminded him. "But I didn't, did I? So when I say you've got to stop disassociating—"

"'Disassociating'?" It was Owen who stood now, and he headed for the doorway. "What's that supposed to mean?"

"You don't want to talk about the fire, you don't want to face Jerry's widow or visit the station, let alone think about going back there to work."

"Are you calling me a coward?"

"No, of course not, but—"

"Because the lily-livered one is you, darling. Making up stories about your perfect family life. Telling tales that aren't true so you can keep *me* out of *your* head."

Her heart stuttered. "This is not about—"

"You married me but you couldn't even

commit to twelve hours as my wife before you had to run away." Owen's blue eyes burned. "I know why now, though, don't I? You just told me. You just told me that you have to keep all your belongings close so you don't leave anything behind by mistake."

"Owen…"

"I was a damned fool that day for believing I'd found the woman I wanted to marry and whom I'd love for the rest of my life. It had only been three days, a Las Vegas weekend, but I was willing to gamble my future on you Izzy. Yeah. I certainly was a chump."

She swallowed. "Owen…"

"Because you're too afraid to take that same kind of chance. You'll never risk your heart, will you, Izzy? You'll never let anyone close enough to touch it."

* * *

She left. She took that suitcase of hers—all packed up as if she'd planned this all along—and walked out on him. Owen couldn't blame her—

Hell, yes, he blamed her!

But he wasn't surprised. After all, after Vegas he'd figured her to be his once and future runaway bride. Going after her was an option, but what was the use? He might think himself in love with her, but she didn't want to be married to him. And hell, after how he'd failed Jerry, Owen wasn't sure what he wanted for himself.

But he wasn't a coward. Shoving his hand through his hair, he nursed his bad temper and thought of all the ways that Izzy had been wrong about him.

He hadn't been distancing himself from the fire. It was all too real, every day, every minute in his head. Where did she think his survivor's guilt came from?

Oh, yeah, he knew what it was. And he was aware he was experiencing it. So he tried telling himself it was the fire that was at fault for Jerry's death. Sometimes he believed it. Other times, he couldn't understand how all their training, their physical fitness, their equipment couldn't have made a difference and kept that young man, that young man about to be a father, alive.

It was then that he couldn't imagine going back to the job that he'd loved because he couldn't believe in the point of it any longer. He didn't have faith that his actions could make a difference.

And he was afraid there wasn't a person or a way to talk himself out of that feeling. Even Izzy, even thinking that he was in love with Izzy, hadn't budged that bleak shadow on his soul.

The doorbell rang.

Izzy? God, he couldn't stop himself from hoping it was her, because even though she'd run over his heart twice on her rush to get out of his life, the stupid thing was still beating.

He wasn't fleet on his feet, but he hurried as quick as he could, flinging open the door to see Jerry's widow. Ellie Palmer.

Hell. He hadn't thought she'd be arriving. After the argument, he'd assumed Izzy would call Ellie and renege on the invitation.

But here she was, looking pale. A small smile curved her lips. "Hi, Owen."

"Hi. I—" What could he say—"Come in"—but that?

The very, very pregnant woman's movements were slow as she crossed the threshold and gingerly sat down on the chair he indicated. She tugged the hem of her maternity dress toward her knees as her gaze roamed the room. "Um, Izzy invited me over."

"Right, right." Shoving his hand through his hair, he took a seat on the sofa opposite her. "She had to step out."

"Oh. Will she be gone long?"

"I'm not sure." *Probably for the rest of my life.* "What I can do is have her call you when she, uh, gets back."

She shook her head. "It was you I wanted

to talk to anyway." Her hand smoothed over the huge bump of her belly. "Do you think I could have a glass of water?"

"Oh, sure. I'm sorry…can I also get you something to eat?"

"No." She grimaced. "I couldn't eat. The water sounds great, though."

He limped away. "Coming right up."

She watched him as he returned from the kitchen and crossed the living room with her glass. "You're moving around pretty well."

"Yeah." Jerry wasn't moving at all. She didn't say the words, but Owen heard them in his head anyway. "And you, you're feeling all right?"

Her free hand, the one without the water glass, rubbed her stomach again. "Okay. Sort of like an overstuffed olive, though."

He managed a laugh at her little joke. "You have family coming to help when the baby's born?"

She nodded. "My mom and dad. Maybe I'll move closer to them afterward. I'm not certain." When she brought her water to her mouth, he noticed her hand was shaking.

Nerves because she was talking to him? "Are you sure you're feeling okay, Ellie?"

"I just want to tell you about Jerry. About how much he liked working with you."

"Oh." *Oh, God.*

"He always said you were the calmest in a crisis. The guy he liked by his side when things were heating up."

"I couldn't save him." The words came from the deepest pit of Owen's belly. "I'm so damn sorry, Ellie. I didn't see, I didn't know, I wish…I so wish…" He closed his eyes, replaying it all again. The darkness, the fire, Jerry's grin. The memory stung his eyes and he squeezed them tighter.

Owen could remember the details clearly now, every one. He saw that truth, that there had been nothing he could do to forestall Jerry's death, but the fact of it still clawed at him. "Ellie…"

Glass shattered.

He jolted, his eyes flying open. Across from him, the pregnant woman was standing, broken glass at her feet. Wetness stained her maternity dress.

"Don't move," he cautioned, rising. "I'll clean up the water and the glass, but I don't want you to risk getting cut."

She was looking at him, her eyes round.

"That's not all that happened. I got to my feet and…"

"And…? Ah." Understanding dawned. "Your water broke."

Her head bobbed up and down in agreement. "I…oh, boy." Her hands clutched at her belly.

Owen hurried to her. Contraction pains already? "Deep breaths, Ellie. Deep breaths."

Her eyes widened. "It's really hurting."

"I know," he said, keeping his voice soothing. "Let's get you down the hall. There's a bedroom in there where you can lie down while I find some dry things for you to wear and call your doctor."

She held his arm as they made the few steps down the hall and then squeezed tighter, causing them both to halt as another contraction hit. "Um…"

He kept his gaze on hers and breathed in and out, trying to silently encourage her to do the same. "You're okay," he said softly. "You're okay."

When the pain passed, he moved as quick as he could, hurriedly laying down some towels when she protested about getting onto the bed. Then he went upstairs to retrieve a T-shirt and sweat pants, and helped her back up and toward the bathroom where she could change.

She had another contraction on the way in, interrupting her recitation of her doctor's name and phone number. Before he'd even had a chance to dial it, the bathroom door was back open. Ellie stood there, in only his big T-shirt, which fell all the way to her knees.

"Um…Owen…" There was a clammy sweat on her face, and when he reached for her, she grabbed on to his fingers in a viselike grip.

As he helped her stretch back out on the bed, he decided that dialing 911 was a sounder idea.

When he hung up the phone, she was having yet another contraction. "Owen," her voice was faint. "I think…I think…"

He squeezed her hands. "Don't worry. I know how to deliver a baby, though I'm sure the paramedics will—"

"Owen!" her voice rose to a breathless squeak. "I think the baby's coming."

"All right. Keep breathing, honey." He met her gaze. "Do you want me to check?"

She nodded vigorously, and then her back bowed as another pain overtook her.

In the bathroom he found another big towel to give her modesty. When it was draped over her legs, he tucked into the kitchen where he thoroughly washed his good hand and wrapped plastic wrap around his cast and other fingers. Then he returned to the bedroom and gently positioned Ellie in order to assess the situation.

Good Lord. He glanced up to see her anxious gaze on his face and flashed her a reassuring smile. "Well, you might want to prepare yourself for a boy who doesn't have much patience for authority figures. I don't think he's going to wait for the EMTs to arrive."

The corners of her mouth quirked in an answering smile. "Like father, like son."

Alexander Gerald Palmer slid into Owen's waiting hands like he was a football delivered by an extremely proficient center. He didn't share that little tidbit with the baby's mother, but as he placed the infant on Ellie's chest, he thought he felt Jerry's presence somewhere, grinning with approval.

That damn grin of Jerry's. Unforgettable.

But he and Ellie were grinning, too, he realized. She shared hers with him and then went back to crooning to the baby. Owen enjoyed the sight for a moment, then heard the commotion at his front door.

Grateful to give the reins over to the personnel who did this kind of thing on a more regular basis, Owen let them in, then retreated to his kitchen while they checked out mother and child. He wasn't alone long. Word must have gotten out, because soon Will and others from the station were milling about his living area, anxious to hear the news.

"I'm telling you," Owen said to his friends. "It's Jerry's boy. He came into the world whistling."

"You look like you're ready to warble something yourself," Will answered. "I haven't seen you smiling like that since… since before."

The comment didn't dissipate Owen's exuberance. "I don't just feel good. I feel great." His training had been worth something again. When the moment came he'd found faith in his ability to handle the situation and help Jerry's widow while she did the important work of birthing her baby. It did make a man want to whistle. Maybe sing a few bars of misheard lyrics.

Yeah. *Hold me closer, Tony Danza.*

He swallowed a laugh and reveled in how damn good it was to delight in being alive.

Chapter Twelve

"There's a lesson to be learned in all this, right?" Izzy said into her cell phone. She moved about the anonymous hotel room, opening her suitcase by rote, as she pondered why burnt orange seemed to be the favorite color of all business-hotel interior designers throughout the country.

"That you can't run away from your

problems?" Emily questioned. "Though I think the nuns in *The Sound of Music* trademarked that one."

"No." Izzy frowned. The bedside alarm clock was a model she wasn't familiar with. Tack on five minutes to make sure she figured out its mechanics.

Oh, but that's right, she didn't have anywhere to be at any particular time. Not for another week.

"I think the lesson here is that a woman shouldn't get married in Las Vegas."

"Worked out pretty well for me," Emily reminded her.

Izzy sighed. "Okay, maybe that *I* shouldn't get married."

"Period? Or just in Nevada?"

She didn't dare answer the question. She

just kept moving about the hotel room, performing her usual tasks: turning back the bedspread and blankets; pulling the light filter curtain so the room wasn't too bright yet wasn't too dark, either; unfurling the towels in the bathroom from their decorative, yet inconvenient, snail-like design.

"Izzy?"

"I'm here." She gazed around the room, trying to figure out something to do with herself next. All her usual make-herself-comfortable actions were complete. Unless she suddenly changed course and developed an itch to unpack—as if that was going to happen—then she was out of busy work. Except…

Sitting herself at the desk, she reached into its drawer for the complimentary stationery and pen she knew she'd find there. "Tell me everything you know about a Nevada annulment."

"Izzy…" There was a wealth of doubt in her friend's voice.

"Please spare me the warning or the lecture or whatever it is you're about to say. I need something to occupy my mind, and the annulment has now found its way to the top of my agenda."

"I didn't look into it with much diligence," Emily confessed.

"That's okay. I just need a starting point."

"Until it's actually granted, you shouldn't enter any beauty pageants."

"What?" The answer startled a laugh out of her, though she wasn't finding much amusing about the past hours of her life.

"You've got to be single to enter most contests like that, and even a quickie wedding in Vegas can mess up your reign if you win."

Izzy held the phone away from her ear for a moment and frowned at it. "What are you talking about?"

"Just one of the pitfalls of research librarianship. I start pulling on a thread and it leads me to the darnedest places."

"Let me get this straight." Izzy rubbed at her forehead. "You were looking into how to end your marriage to Will and you found out about beauty contest rules?"

"I told you, I didn't look into it with much diligence."

"I'll say."

"Hey," Emily defended herself. "You have the same skills that I do, and you've managed to not even find out that much. At least I had the excuse of being in love with my husband and in my heart of hearts not wanting the marriage to be over at all. What's yours?"

"I'm not in love with Owen!" She heard the strident tone in her voice and tried too late to calm it. "I can't be in love with Owen."

"Okay, okay," Emily soothed. "Relax. I remember a little bit more about the annulment rules. If one or both of you is under eighteen without a parent's consent, the marriage can be annulled. Bigamy gets you out of it. Consanguination."

Since they both were thirty, never married before and not related by blood, those were all out. "What else?"

"Drug or alcohol addiction."

"I don't wish for either one of those. Is there another circumstance?"

"Hmm…I think if the marriage was the result of threat or duress."

Izzy pursed her lips and tried imagining the scene. *Your honor, this man's kisses put me under such duress that I didn't hesitate to say "I do."* She sighed. "Do you have anything else?"

"Well…" Emily was quiet a moment. "Fraud might do it."

"Fraud?"

"Yes. You tell the judge Owen misrepresented himself somehow. There was a famous celebrity marriage that ended in just over fifty hours when a pop singer convinced the judge that she and her nongroom hadn't had an honest discussion of where they would live or if they wanted kids, that sort of thing."

Izzy penned the word on her piece of paper. *F-R-A-U-D*. Then she wrote it how Melvil Dewey might have. *F-R-O-D*. Then she crossed them both out.

It was true that they'd never discussed where they might live or anything about children. But… "There's no one less a fraud in the western half of the United States than Owen Marston," she said. "He's a firefighter, for goodness sake. The kind of man who devotes his career to helping others. Every day he's out there saving lives and property."

Okay, she knew she was preaching to the choir, because Emily's husband, Will, was just such a person, too, but she couldn't let the words go unsaid. She rose from the desk chair to pace about the room. "I could never stand before anyone and tell them Owen was a fraud."

"Okay," Emily said again. "I get you on that. But Izzy…"

There was a note in her friend's voice that told her a lightbulb had gone off. Emily, bless her fact-finding little heart, had thought of something.

"What?" she demanded. "But what?"

"Are you sitting down?"

Izzy huffed in impatience, but she threw herself onto the end of the bed. "Yes. Now out with it."

"Well, Iz," Emily said slowly. "What about Owen going before the judge and testifying that the one in this marriage who perpetrated a fraud was you?"

Izzy's stomach whooshed to her toes. She tightened her fingers on the phone and pressed the flat of her other hand to the mattress. "Me? Why would you think he would say that about me?"

"You weren't really serious about the marriage at all, were you?" Emily asked.

"I don't know why—"

"You were scuttling from the hotel when dawn broke."

Izzy's breath didn't seem to reach her lungs. "You left Las Vegas, too," she pointed out.

"I tried to contact Will. And I knew that I was going to be living just a few miles from him. He knew he was going to be able to find me. You didn't even give Owen your cell phone number."

Because she was scared! Because she was

scared that if she heard his voice she'd be seduced again by the fantasy of all that she'd learned never to believe in. A man, a marriage, a family that didn't just see her as an inconvenience or an obligation.

How could she trust that? How many times when she was five or eight or ten had she let herself think that her current caretaker loved her and wanted her and would love her and want her forever? Each time she'd been disappointed when a different car would drive up and she'd be shuffled to yet another person who didn't really care.

There at the new place she'd turn on the charm, she'd make herself small or quiet or helpful, whatever was required, and yet it still was never enough.

She had never been enough.

"Izzy? Izzy, you know I love you."

"Yes," she said dully. "Yes, I know that." She had found good, close friends, and she cherished them, though truth to tell, even they weren't the same as what she'd pretended for three days in Las Vegas that she could have with Owen.

"So you know I don't like saying this," Emily continued. "But I'm right, aren't I? It was you who went to the altar under false pretenses."

"Yes," she said again.

"You didn't believe in a lifetime with the man."

"Yes," she agreed again.

"And you weren't the least bit in love with him."

Izzy took a breath. The agreement to that sentence just sat on her tongue.

"Iz?"

She stayed silent.

"You weren't in love with him, right?" Emily insisted. "You *aren't* in love with him, right?"

Wrong.

Izzy put her head in her hand. She'd been wrong about so many things, but it was too late…for her and Owen.

And for her crumbling heart.

At the sound of the doorbell, Owen continued his phone conversation with Will. He pulled open the front door to find his brother, whom he gestured inside. "I'll work shifts for you. I'll cut your damn lawn for a month. Just get me her cell phone number."

Will started to hem and haw, but Owen interrupted him. "She walked out on me. And took my car. For God's sake, I at least need to demand my ride back."

Bryce waved his hand in Owen's face. "You need Izzy's cell phone number?"

Cupping his hand over the phone, he addressed his brother. "Yeah. And don't say anything about me being stupid not to have it. I get that."

Bryce grinned. "But *I* have *it.*"

"Never mind, Will," Owen said into the phone, hanging up and looking at his brother expectantly, his fingers hovering over the keypad. "Go ahead."

Grinning, Bryce dropped onto the couch

and stretched out his legs. "Wait a minute. Aren't we going to negotiate? You were offering to cut Will's lawn."

"I'll cut important parts of your body off if you don't give it to me right now."

"Ouch." Still grinning, Bryce crossed his legs. "But c'mon, bro, I do you a favor, you do me a favor…"

Owen took a breath. "Fine. Here's the favor—I'm not going to join the family company, where I would have swiftly risen in the ranks to become your boss and then taken great pleasure in canning your irritating ass."

Bryce sat up straight. "Really?"

"Really. So thank me for saving your career by giving me Isabella's phone number."

His brother dug in his front pocket for his

phone. "I see a man retaking control of his life."

"Yeah." He paused, then felt his mouth curve in a smile like it had been doing about every fifteen minutes since the day before, when Alexander Gerald Palmer made his way into the world. "I helped deliver a baby yesterday."

"No kidding. Anybody's I know?"

"Jerry's wife. Jerry's son." It still felt damn good to know that he'd been able to help Jerry's widow. The experience had given Owen back his juice, the motivation and the energy to return to the work that was his life's calling.

And the motivation, energy and determination to try to get a certain wife to return to his life, too.

The way he figured it, now that his head was finally back in working order, was that Izzy had gone AWOL in Las Vegas because she was afraid to believe they could have a real marriage. But she hadn't disbelieved enough to start proceedings to end it, either. That said something. "Give me the number, Bryce."

His brother rattled it off and Owen punched it into his phone. Then he hesitated, and added the number to his address book instead of directly dialing Izzy. Still considering, he glanced at his brother again.

"I figure you owe me more," he told Bryce.

"What? Why?"

"It's a big thing to save a man's job, not to mention his standing in the family. Look, I'll keep quiet about the emergency birth thing, if you give me a couple hours of your time."

Amusement sparked in Bryce's eyes, but he made a show of grumbling. "Want to make a bet that we'll all be sitting around the turkey at Thanksgiving and you'll somehow let it slip?"

"Right now there's only one thing I'm willing to gamble on," Owen replied.

He wanted his car back. Of course he wanted his car back, Izzy acknowledged. It was mortifying to recall that she'd driven off in it and then never given the vehicle another thought. Her mind had been occupied elsewhere.

She was in love with Owen, and she'd blown it.

The worst thing about the situation, she thought, as she pulled into his driveway, was that even if she could replay the last four weeks, she didn't see herself doing anything differently.

You could know that you were in love.

You could see that you'd had a chance at something you'd never expected to touch.

But you could still be unable to make yourself reach out and grasp it.

Her foot caught on a pile of flattened empty boxes stacked against the garage and she gave them a little kick before marching toward the front door. It felt like an execution was in the offing, but she wasn't going to let him know that this meeting would be the lethal injection to her heart.

It wasn't his fault that she couldn't be the

kind of woman he deserved. She could work at being friendly, fun and pleasing, but for the life and marriage he wanted she had to be trusting and open. For too long she'd only had herself to rely on, and she couldn't see herself learning to rely on someone else.

As she reached the front door, it suddenly opened. She took a hasty step back, then saw that it was Bryce, who looked a little sweaty and dusty. He smiled, then swooped in to grab her up for a kiss on the forehead. "Later, little fairy," he said, then breezed past her at a jog.

She gazed after him with a sad smile. "I didn't get a chance to say goodbye," she murmured to his retreating back. It was likely she'd never see him again.

"Tears?" a voice said at her back. "Don't tell me you're crying over my little brother."

She blinked rapidly and then spun around. "Of course not." There was going to be no sentiment during this meeting. She'd hand over the keys and they'd exchange thoughts on how best to end their marriage.

Owen backed away from the threshold. "Come inside."

On the small table in the shallow foyer was a huge arrangement of pale-blue roses. Maybe two dozen. She stared at the flowers, wondering who had sent them, and then immediately thought of single mom Alicia. Had she stepped up her courtship of Owen despite Izzy's laying claim to him?

Or had he called the other woman and explained their not-really-a-marriage himself?

"They're from Ellie Palmer's parents," he said, his gaze on her face. "Yesterday, during the visit you arranged, we had a surprise special delivery on these very premises."

Izzy's eyes widened as she deduced his meaning. "What? The baby? Born here?"

"Yep." He smiled. "The baby. Born here."

"Wow. They're okay?"

"They're okay. I'm okay."

She studied the relaxed expression on his face. He looked different. Happy. Purposeful. The tightness in her chest eased a little. It appeared as if the old Owen—the man she'd married—was back.

"Let's sit down for a minute," he said.

Following him in, she tried breathing slow and easy. He sat on the couch, and she took the chair opposite. Something seemed different, besides his newly relaxed demeanor, but she couldn't quite put her finger on it. Frowning, she reached out to place his keys on the table between them. "Sorry about taking off with your car."

"No problem." He scooped up the metal ring and immediately pocketed it.

She frowned again, annoyed with herself for not thinking to call a cab to pick her up here at a certain time. Now she'd have to have Owen drive her back to the hotel or stand around on his sidewalk while she waited for a taxi once they were through.

Oh, well. She wiped her palms on her thighs and took a quick breath. "We should talk."

He nodded. "We should."

She looked down at her hands as a silence

stretched between them. "I've started looking into the annulment laws."

"Yeah? Me, too."

Why did that hurt so much? She twisted her fingers together. "There's a couple of possibilities."

"No. No, there's not."

Her gaze jumped up to meet his. His expression was unreadable, but his face was so handsome and so…so *dear* to her. How had this happened? How had she been so stupid as to fall in love when she was the kind of person who couldn't let herself count on forever?

"The annulment idea won't work," Owen said.

"Oh, but I think we can find something in our circumstance that fits—"

"We've been living together, Izzy. I admit I'm no legal expert, but from what I've read, the fact that we've been living together—and sleeping together—puts the kibosh on that plan."

She slumped against the back of the chair. Yesterday, after her conversation with Emily during which she'd confronted the truth that she was in love with Owen, she'd stopped thinking about a way out of their marriage and just wallowed in self-pity.

And really bad room-service pizza.

She held her palm to her stomach as if it were still burning a hole there. "Really? There's a clause about living together?"

Owen nodded. "Think so."

Her eyes closed. That meant they needed a divorce then. The idea of it only served to wound her ready-to-be-executed heart. An annulment could be something to forget about, since it legally ruled that the marriage had indeed never occurred. But a divorce made it real.

A divorce made it real that she'd wedded the man she was in love with and that she didn't have what it took to stay married to him. Bryce had once called her a woman who made do with less. Had he been right?

"Izzy," Owen said softly. "Isabella."

She willed away the tears stinging her eyes. Swallowing hard, she looked at him. "What is it?"

"Izzy..."

Her gaze snagged on a quilt folded over the arm of the sofa he was sitting on. It looked familiar. She frowned at it, then scooted forward on her cushion so she had a better view. It certainly was a quilt. In the colors of her alma mater. The alma mater she shared with Emily.

As a matter of fact, it appeared to be the very quilt that Emily had made for Izzy the year after they'd graduated.

Eyebrows raised, she looked at Owen. He was watching her, and something in his expression made her run her gaze around the room. Some of the firefighter memorabilia on the bookcase had been re-arranged. There were more books on the shelves now, including *Eight Cousins* and *A Rose in Bloom*.

Her books.

She rose to her feet, her insides unsteady as she toured the house. In the kitchen were some hand-embroidered tea towels that one of her *zias* had given her when she turned eighteen. Down the hall, in the room Owen used as a home office, her framed college diplomas hung on the wall next to his. Photographs that she'd taken over the years were set about, too. With a tentative fingertip, she touched one. It wasn't a figment of her imagination.

Then she whirled, sensing Owen behind her. He stood in the doorway, his gaze trained on her face. She looked away, because what she was feeling was too big, too scary, too hard to speak of. He moved aside as she approached the door and then trailed her up the stairs to the next level.

In his bedroom, she found the clothes that had been in boxes in the garage hanging in the closet. A pair of scruffy slippers shaped like jalapeño peppers that she'd had since high school and never gotten around to throwing out peeked from under the bed.

Owen cleared his throat. "There were some god-awful flannel granny nightgowns. I took the liberty of tossing those."

She still couldn't look at him. Her gaze hit on another familiar item. It was propped on the pillows in the center of the bed. One of her friends had embroidered the heart-shaped thing for her eons ago. "My night has become a sunny dawn because of you."

Blinking rapidly, she turned her head, only to find something that sent the tears cascading down her cheeks. On the bedside table—on the side that *he* slept on—was a beautiful frame. And inside it—their marriage certificate.

Her gaze jumped to her side of the bed, and there, in a matching frame, was a photograph from their wedding. Magnetlike, it drew her, and she took it in her hand, her vision blurring so that she couldn't see the image of the two people who had found each other through some unexplainable intersection of luck and fate.

It didn't matter. She remembered exactly how the couple had felt.

Happy. In love. Ready to face the future together.

She wiped her face with the back of her hand and then looked over at her husband. He was smiling at her, and she guessed that he knew his gesture had been the exact right thing to get through to her. The exact right thing to make her believe.

"You made a place for me here," she said.

"Because I want you in my life," Owen answered. "Forever. Do you think the rolling stone can settle down awhile?"

She sniffed, and had to wipe at her wet face again. She'd lived nowhere because there'd been no one she'd felt like this about. "I like Paxton. You know I'm in love with you."

Grinning now, he came closer. "I counted on it." He placed the photograph back on the table and then took her into his arms.

"I can count on you." The knowledge was the sunny dawn that warmed every lonely and empty corner of her soul. After a childhood filled with unreliability, it was this that she needed. To know that she could count on him. He'd proved it to her, hadn't he, by putting her things side by side with his. "I can really, really count on you."

"Yes. On my support, on my partnership. On my love."

Izzy hugged Owen to her, hearing his heart beating steady in her ear. "I am going to make you so happy," she said fiercely. "Wait until you see how stubborn I can be about that."

He tipped her face up for his kiss. "No more running?"

"Only to you," she answered. "Always."

* * * * *

millsandboon.co.uk Community
Join Us!

The Community is the perfect place to meet and chat to kindred spirits who love books and reading as much as you do, but it's also the place to:

- **Get the inside scoop from authors about their latest books**
- **Learn how to write a romance book with advice from our editors**
- **Help us to continue publishing the best in women's fiction**
- **Share your thoughts on the books we publish**
- **Befriend other users**

Forums: Interact with each other as well as authors, editors and a whole host of other users worldwide.

Blogs: Every registered community member has their own blog to tell the world what they're up to and what's on their mind.

Book Challenge: We're aiming to read 5,000 books and have joined forces with The Reading Agency in our inaugural Book Challenge.

Profile Page: Showcase yourself and keep a record of your recent community activity.

Social Networking: We've added buttons at the end of every post to share via digg, Facebook, Google, Yahoo, technorati and de.licio.us.

www.millsandboon.co.uk